You will love *The Canary* if you are literarily inclined and still deeply care about how people think and feel, and what motivates the human heart.

~Monique Raphel High,
author of *Between Two Worlds*

**Other Books by Michael Loyd Gray**

*Well Deserved,* 2009, Sol Books (Winner of the 2008 Sol Books Prose Series Prize)

*Not Famous Anymore,* 2012, Three Towers Press

*King Biscuit,* 2012, Tempest Books

Bottom Dog Press

Amelia
Earhart
c. 1917

Ernest
Hemingway
c. 1916

# The Canary

## A Novel

Michael Loyd Gray

"Myths are made for the imagination
to put life into them."
~Albert Camus

Harmony Series
Bottom Dog Press
Huron, Ohio

ISBN 978-1-933964-73-7
Bottom Dog Publishing
PO Box 425
Huron, Ohio 44839
http://smithdocs.net
e-mail: Lsmithdog@smithdocs.net

First Edition

**This is a work of fiction.**

**Credits:**
General Editor: Larry Smith
Cover Design: Susanna Sharp-Schwacke
Cover Art: Amelia Earhart © Suzanne Gee
www.suzannegee.com
Photographs:
Young Ernest Hemingway: Ernest Hemingway Collection. John F. Kennedy Presidential Library and Museum, Boston
Young Amelia Earhart: The Amelia Earhart Museum
http://www.ameliaearhart.com/museum/
Author photo on cover: Cindy Pringle

Dedication

This book is for Pauline Vilain, E.H., and Moonpie.
Gone but never will they be forgotten.

*Courage*

Courage is the price which life exacts for granting peace.
The soul that knows it not, knows no release
From little things;
Knows not the livid loneliness of fear
Nor mountain heights, where bitter joy you can hear
The sound of wings.
How can life grant us boon of living, compensate,
For dull gray ugliness and pregnant hate
Unless we dare
The soul's dominion? Each time we make a choice we pay
With courage to behold resistless day
And count it fair.

~ *Amelia Earhart*

# Air

The comforting drone of engines.

Humming.

A limitless blue horizon.

Lift buoying wings.

Fuel pumping from tanks.

Blood coursing veins.

Flooding arteries.

Sweaty palms gripping.

Clutching.

*"KHAQQ calling Itasca...We must be on you, but cannot see you – but gas is running low. Have been unable to reach you by radio. We are flying at 1,000 feet."*

Scattered clouds.

Dark shadows on the ocean's surface.

Obscuring.

*"We are on the line 157 337. We will repeat this message. We will repeat this on 6210 kilocycles. Wait. We are running on line north and south."*

## Grounded

*Down. But hard. Alive. But a bang and a screech.*

*A hardscrabble reef on a pipsqueak island that materialized as thirsty engines drank last gulps, sputtered, failed. A shallow reef barely resembling anything at all a pilot would call a place to land.*

*A speck floating on the ocean at first glance.*

*Even at second glance.*

*There was no time for a third glance.*

*It was nothing to write home about.*

*But all there was.*

*You take what you can get.*

*You take what's there.*

*But it wasn't much.*

*My head ached to look at it.*

*But I took it.*

*Lord, I did.*

*Any pilot would.*

*I'm a pilot.*

*This landing proves it.*

*But the impact collapsed a landing gear and I'm sitting here now in the sand but with the shade of a palm tree. I'm looking at my broken bird, one wing down in the water.*

*Together we are birds chirping a sad, lonely song.*

*Mostly I'm doing the chirping.*

*Such a sad, lonely song.*

*My bird: Lockheed Electra 10E. A broken bird.*

*But we got down. Safe. Rib rattling, but safe.*

*As abrupt a landing as I can imagine or would ever want to make again. A teeth-rattling plop out of the sky.*

*Fell like a stone.*

*Nothing like the time I put the Kinner Airster down a bit heavily in Cora Kinner's cabbage patch in California.*

*This landing was abrupt and belligerent. We were out of gas, out of options, and out of sight of the world. Gravity assumed command.*

*We fell to earth from the sky.*

*And found a damn reef.*

*Bounced along its angry teeth.*

*But damn if we didn't get her down on this godforsaken reef on this godforsaken island in the middle of this godforsaken ocean.*

*Any landing you walk away from is a good one.*

*So they say.*

*A godforsaken saying, if you ask me.*

*But no one's asking.*

*Well, anyway – we walked away. Limped away. Crawled away. My knee is bruised. Hurts like the dickens. It collided with something metal. And there's a nice bump on my forehead – more collision. I know I look a fright. I'm glad I have no mirror.*

*Fred's back is wrenched. He's in the grove of trees behind me, just a few yards away, resting as best he can. But not doing well. Not at all. I heard him moan a moment ago.*

*Fred's a broken bird, too.*

*Who will mend his wings?*

*And mine?*

## Wingless

*The Electra, my old friend, my grand girl – gone.*

*Snatched.*

*Swept out from the reef into the depths. I watched with tears from the shade of a palm tree. Farewell, lovely one. I was your witness and I cried as you were torn away. Pulled under. Ripped from me by an angry sea.*

*You sleep now far below.*

*I helped Fred sit up so he could watch, too. He cried and patted my shoulder. He whispered sweet things, despite his pain, to try and soothe me.*

*Sweet, broken bird, take your leave and rest forever.*

*Fly beneath the waves as well as you did in the sky.*

*But I know better than to believe that.*

*I wish it.*

*Not the same thing.*

*You served me well, broken bird. I served you badly. I could not save you. But no blame to you. Much to me. I loved you. Truly. I could never blame you.*

*The failure was many things: Liquid – fuel.*

*Navigation – unfortunate.*

*Communications – failed.*

*Bad luck.*

*Luck is a factor.*

*Make your own luck.*

*I tried.*

*I always tried.*

*Easier said than done.*

*Fuel runs out.*

*So does luck.*

# Rare as Gold

*I have become a good hunter of birds and turtles. Crabs, too. But the crabs are creeping, pinching troops. An enemy army. Fred says they're coconut crabs. But they're an army nonetheless. Who will win this fight? So far, it's me.*

*They are endless, the crabs. Swarming dots at a distance. Tiny, creeping monsters up close. But they have moisture. Wondrous moisture – now more valuable than gold. Gold would mean nothing here. Moisture – what we can eat has moisture. And rainwater collects in the crooks of trees.*

*Rare as gold.*

*Gold would mean nothing here.*

*What does matter here? Water. Water is gold. Rain is life. Life out of life.*

*The bodies of crabs, turtles, birds moisten us. Their moisture becomes our moisture. Flows into our water. Becomes our water. A circle of life. They become a part of us. Are we part of them?*

*The senses dull in the stifling heat and relentless – sameness.*

*We nap. A deep stupor, really. How many days? Perhaps five or six or even more, I think. And I think some more, sluggishly, and count some more, like a young girl just learning numbers. My smile is thin.*

*A birthday approaches. The twenty-fourth of July. My fortieth.*

*Well, numbers mean nothing here.*

*An old wreck rusts offshore. A steamer of some sort. It had bad luck, too. Welcome to Bad Luck Island. But I mustn't think that way. Yet, sometimes I wake thinking: The shipwreck is the Itasca, come to save us.*

*So insistent to save us it beaches itself.*

*Grinds onto the reef.*

*Rescuers pour from it like angry ants.*

*But I blink and the rescuers are just gulls.*

*The ship does not move.*

*Will not move.*

*Cannot move.*

*Only I can move.*

*From one end of the atoll to the other.*

*Or to the lagoon, where we often catch birds, turtles.*

*And find water in the crooks of trees.*

*But I was too slow this day.*

*Deep in my stupor in the shade of trees.*

*Fred, too.*

*Deep into dreams and nightmares, the lines blurry.*

*And then I heard the sound of insects.*

*Had heard it many times before.*

*Insistent insects.*

*A buzzing.*

*In my stupor it got louder.*

*As if the insects had grown.*

*Mutated into great insect beasts.*

*With silver wings.*

*Capable of rattling the palm trees when they flew by.*

*Roaring along the surf to the far end of the atoll.*

*Roaring back, even lower.*

*Swoosh!*

*Funny, those giant insects.*

*I instinctively swat at them and the motion wakes me.*

*I come back to reality.*

*I see and hear too late.*

*I stumble slowly from the shelter of the trees.*

*Onto the beach.*

*Just in time to see them roar away.*

*Three of them.*

*Navy planes.*

*Looking for me.*

*Here I am.*

*Amelia.*

*The one you seek.*

*Can you see me?*

*Come back.*

*But the giant insects do not.*

*They disappear into the endless horizon.*

*Perhaps to Howland?*

*Surely they know the way.*

*Come back, insects.*

*I am Amelia.*

# Mid-Day

Latitude 4 43 39 S.
Longitude 174 31 23 W.

Palm trees cast thin shadows on a white beach.

*Fred is dead.*

Palm fronds scrape each other.

*Fred is dead.*

Turbulent surf falls, foams.

*Fred is dead.*

A breeze rises, breaks, falls.

*Fred is dead.*

Gulls circle lazily.

*Fred is dead.*

Humidity creeps, dampens.

*Fred Noonan is dead.*

*Now I sleep a while.*

# Chicago

*It's so hot that I easily dream of the past:*

I am walking around Hyde Park.
We have just moved to Chicago.
1914.
Early fall.
What a place!
People everywhere.
Lots of tall buildings.
A far cry from Atchison.

It's lovely outdoors and leaves are red and yellow on the trees. A gentle breeze wanders in from Lake Michigan and ruffles the leaves ever so slightly. Lake Michigan is blue, immense, but calm. An inland ocean at rest.

I have started school at Hyde Park High and will graduate high school a Chicagoan. I never would have imagined that. Well, not truly a Chicagoan. A transplant. And still a Kansan. But we are here, in the Windy City, because mother has left father and we are determined to make it on our own. His drinking had become impossible. Father went off to Kansas City, to see what he might yet make of himself. So, here we are, in exciting Chicago.

Originally I was to attend Morgan Park High. But Morgan Park High was unsuitable. Really rather poor facilities. Why, the chemistry lab was nothing at all. Like a little kitchen lacking proper utensils, I should say. But Hyde Park High is different. It excels at the sciences and those are my interests. I am told Hyde Park High is the best public school. And it's near that great University of Chicago. Bright and creative people abound. At night I spend time caring for mother, who feels poorly these days. But after school I sometimes steal away to see some of Chicago.

South Water Street—incredible congestion: horse-drawn wagons and motor trucks hauling produce for market. Store awnings stretching endlessly down the street. People and animals sending dust clouds and smells into the air. And State Street—all those men in yellow skimmer hats and ladies in floppy hats of all colors. And the trolleys—but more horse-drawn wagons and carts, too. And Union Station and huge brick buildings across the street. One emblazoned with a huge advertisement for Coca-Cola—Drink Coca-Cola to Relieve Fatigue.

I'm not tired at all!

One Sunday I eat at a small diner on Michigan Avenue. Funny that I don't recall the name now. A large sign hung above the doorway. Anyway, it was sunny and cool but not cold. I'm at a stool at the counter, near the door, and the seat next to me is open, but there are people all along the rest of the counter and filling the booths and it's quite busy—lunchtime. The sound of plates and silverware and glasses striking tables and counters reverberates throughout the diner. I chuckle at the sound of a cook bellowing orders in the kitchen.

A boy younger than I comes in and pauses a moment in the doorway. Unsure, perhaps, whether he wants to be here? I notice only because when the door opens a bell rings and it's instinctive to look. The boy is handsome and wearing one of those hats many boys wear, though I can't seem to name it. A newsboy cap? I'm not sure. The boy slips the hat off and his dark hair tumbles out and hangs a little over his forehead. He sweeps it back with a hand and then he grins and the grin is rather magnificent. It seems to fill the room. And makes me smile, too. This boy is about five-nine, I judge, and sort of lean—but not skinny. He seems athletic and quite solid on his feet. He's wearing dark trousers and a dark jacket over a dark sweatshirt—is there no color in his life?

He takes a few steps and then notices the stool next to me and hesitates. He looks around the diner again and then at the stool and at me and we make eye contact. He flashes that magnificent grin again and I suspect that wherever he goes he is often the focus of attention.

"Can I sit?" he says.

"I don't know," I say, not smiling. "Can you?"

His face flashes indecision, but then the big grin comes back and I must smile, too, and not seem mean. He slides onto the stool and looks quickly over his shoulder back toward the door and the street as though something might be there.

"Are you being followed?" I ask.

"What?" He studies my face a moment. "Oh—no. Having my back to a door makes me nervous, I guess. Superstition."

He shrugs, but there's that magnificent grin again.

"Unless someone is really following you, of course," I say, trying not to smile, but I do anyway.

He glances at the door again.

"Well, I don't see anyone, so I guess we're okay," he says.

"You're quite sure?" I say.

He studies my face again. He can be quite intense.

"What's your name?" he asks.

"Amelia."

His eyebrows arch.

"I've never met an Amelia," he says.

"And now you have."

He laughs. "I guess I have."

"What's *your* name?" I say.

"Ernest."

"I've never met an Ernest."

"Now you have."

We both laugh and he picks up a menu and studies it a moment.

"What did you order?" he says, still studying the menu.

"Chipped beef on toast with gravy and mashed potatoes," I say.

"Are they slow today?" he asks.

"It would seem so. Quite the crowd here, Ernest."

"You can call me Ernie, if you like—or Hem. Or Hemmy."

"Hemmy?"

"How about Hem? My last name is Hemingway."

"I've never known a Hemingway."

"Now you have."

He grins again, satisfied with himself.

"You can also call me Hemingstein."

"So many names," I say. "I'm overwhelmed. Are you so many people?"

The waitress comes and Ernest orders a ham and cheese sandwich and a glass of milk. It's warm inside the diner and he slips off his jacket and drapes it over a knee.

"What were you saying?" Ernest asks.

"I was asking about all your names."

That grin again. Even the young waitress has noticed it and suddenly she is attentive to him. He declines more milk and asks for water.

"So, which name for me have you settled on, Amelia?"

I study him a moment. He's confident. Is it forced? Real?

"I can call you Hem," I say. "How's that?"

"We're off to a great start," he says.

The waitress brings his milk and he takes a huge gulp of it. My beef and potatoes arrive and I dig in. My walk had worked up an appetite. The food rejuvenates me and I have a second cup of coffee.

"Are you in school?" Ernest asks.

"Hyde Park High," I say between bites of beef. "And you?"

"Oak Park High."

"I don't know where that is," I say.

"You don't know where Oak Park is and you're from Chicago?"

"No, I'm not from Chicago," I say. "I came here to finish school. But I'm from Kansas—Atchison."

"You just moved here from Atchison? I have an uncle in Kansas City."

"No, we just moved here from St. Paul. But I grew up in Atchison."

"St. Paul, Minnesota?" he says. "A real world traveler." His sandwich arrives and he takes a big bite and chews happily. A boy who likes to eat.

"Have you always lived in Chicago, Hem?"

The grin again. Clearly he loves attention and the business of so many nicknames. I wonder if even Chicago will be grand enough to contain him.

"I was born in Oak Park," he says. "But we go to northern Michigan every summer. We have a cottage there."

"Where?"

"Walloon Lake."

"It sounds lovely."

"It's amazing," he says. "Our cottage is called Windemere. We have a long rickety dock and a strip of beach shaded by cedars and birches. And there are Indians and endless forests and the fishing is the best. We eat trout cooked over campfires."

I nod and smile. The words seem to tumble from his mouth. A boy who can't get enough of the outdoors and who speaks well.

"In Atchison I lived in a house on a bluff overlooking the Missouri River, Hem."

"Really?" He looks genuinely impressed for a boy who likely is not easily impressed. "I'd like to see the Missouri River. Sometimes my friend Lewis Clarnahan and I hike out to the Des Plaines River and fish for carp on the North Avenue Bridge. I caught the biggest one ever taken there."

I nod, wonder if that's true, realize to Ernest it may be irrelevant.

"A big carp, was it?"

"Huge." He spreads his hands wide apart and clearly is exaggerating, his magnificent grin seeming to widen with his hands.

"I should like to have seen it," I say. "What's your friend Lewis like?"

Hem shrugs.

"I guess he's okay for a guy. We play tennis, too. And do some shooting out on the prairie."

He wipes his hands on a napkin and looks around the room a moment as though aware for the first time he's there. Then he grins at me again but doesn't say anything. I suspect his reserves for merriment and mischiefs are quite deep. There's no denying his likeability.

"Are you a good shot, Hem?"

He nods. "Not bad."

"I can shoot," I say. "When I was growing up in Atchison I hunted rats with a .22 rifle."

Hem looks a little surprised.

"Did you hit any of these rats?"

"I got my share."

He nods approval and grins again.

"Were they rats or rabbits?"

"I know the difference, Hem."

His face gets a sheepish look before the grin comes back.

"I'm sure you do," he says. "You're okay, Amelia. Say—what's your last name?"

I cock my head to the side.

"Can a lady really divulge such information to a stranger?"

"I can be strange, I guess," he says. "But I'm not a stranger—you're calling me Hem. Now we're pals.

I sense that Ernest relishes pals, needs plenty of pals, needs them to orbit him. Maybe even rather lords over pals a bit.

"I'm Amelia Earhart."

He nods some more, seems to weigh the name.

"It suits you," he says. "Amelia Earhart—it has a good cadence to it. Rolls off the tongue just right. That's important with words."

"Are you an authority on words, Hem?"

"Naw. Not really. When were you born?"

I thought that was rather abrupt and I frowned slightly.

"Such a thing for a gentleman to ask a lady," I say.

"I was just asking," he says, shrugging. "I was born on July 21."

"July 24," I say after a long pause.

"Really? That means we're a lot alike."

"Not always," I say.

"Sure it does," he insists playfully. "So, what's it like at Hyde Park High?"

"It's a good school," I say. "Good facilities."

He makes a face.

"But what's it like?" he asks, his voice rising slightly. "What are the people like?"

"Pleasant," I say.

"Pleasant? But what are your friends *like*?"

"I don't have any," I say. "I spend a lot of time looking after Mother."

"Just you and your mother?"

"Yes," I say, looking away a moment.

"What about your father?"

"He's in Kansas City" I say as I turn back toward him and smile bravely. "He's there seeing about work."

"What does he do?"

"He's a lawyer. What does *your* father do, Hem?"

"He's a doctor."

"Really? How nice. Maybe you'll follow his footsteps."

But I didn't really think that's the direction Ernest would choose.

"Maybe," he says. "Who knows."

As always, he relies on the grin.

"What will you do after high school, Amelia?"

"More school, I imagine. As you say—who knows."

"Where will you go?"

"I'm not sure yet," I say. "Maybe in Philadelphia, though."

"Philadelphia?" He seems to mull that. "What's there?"

"Bryn Mawr. I fancy it, Hem."

He nods. "I might go to school down at Illinois. But that's a while off. A lot can happen to change things. That's not set at all."

Although I sensed Ernest was quite bright, I had trouble visualizing him in college. Not for lack of ability, of course. But college seemed too restricting for such a boy. I could imagine him doing something big, but of course I had no idea what that could be. He could even turn out to be a criminal, but a famous one--a modern day Jesse James.

"I must go now, Hem. I have the walk home. And mother will be looking for me."

I gathered my coat and got up. When I put the coat on, Ernest helped me like a true gentleman. He even opened the diner door for me and on the street were many people going by and much noise from conversations and trucks and horse-drawn wagons.

"It was swell to meet you, Amelia."

"Yes—I enjoyed it, Hem."

"Do you come downtown very often?" he asks.

I paused, looked into his wonderful eyes, heard myself say, "When I can. But usually only on a Sunday."

"Maybe we could have lunch together again," he says.

"*Did* we have lunch together, Ernest?"

He frowns slightly.

"Well—sure we did. We sat together."

"You took the last open seat," I say. "It happened to be next to me."

"Fate?" he said, and I sensed this was something Ernest was a big believer in—fate. And perhaps chivalry and other grand notions.

"We did have lunch together," I say. "In a casual sort of way."

"Of course we did," he says. "Can you come downtown again next Sunday?"

"Maybe. But for what purpose—Ernest?"

"Aren't you going to call me Hem anymore?"

"Okay—Hem." He really could be quite irresistible—especially when he rather unfairly flashes the magnificent grin.

He looks up, at the diner's sign over the door, as if to take his bearings.

"We should have lunch here again," he says. "Sunday. And I'll get you to start calling me Hemingstein."

"Are you so sure, Ernest?"

But clearly he is sure that he can accomplish much through the sheer force of his will and presence, which are considerable but raw and undeveloped.

"Call it lunch with a new friend," he says.

I mull the invitation a moment and look at the street, at horses pulling carts.

"I can't promise anything. But I'll try. We'll see."

He beams. "Good enough. About noon, then."

"Perhaps," I say, but I smile. "Well, now I really must go, Ernest."

"Hem."

"Yes—Hem."

I offer a hand and we shake and his hand is warm. Then I turn and walk south on Michigan Avenue. After a few steps I glance back and Ernest is still there, hands on hips, the magnificent grin spreading.

"Hemingstein!" he calls, laughing.

# Midnight

*I wake up abruptly, sweating.*

*Disoriented.*

*But I can see I'm still on this godforsaken island. Calm yourself. I will. Focus. I will.*

*What is this place?*

*An island. Don't be silly – of course, it's an island. But not Howland Island. No. Certainly not. We had this discussion, Fred and I. Fred would not be dead if this were Howland. Fred would be smiling. I would be smiling.*

*The world would be smiling.*

*Would it?*

*And there would be no more crabs. Back home I would ban crabs forever. George would surely understand. George – the good husband.*

*George is doing things now to find me.*

*Cling to that.*

*But this place must surely have a name. Yes – on a chart somewhere. The Itasca surely knows it. Where is the Itasca? Out there – in the endless darkness, endless ocean.*

*But maybe not far at all.*

*No way to know.*

*Itasca – it has a ring to it.*

*Fred Noonan Island.*

*It has a ring to it.*

*Much better than Crab Island.*

*Infinitely better.*

*But I don't want to think about infinity.*

*This is not Infinity Island.*

*I will be asked, of course.*

*Should I survive, that is.*

*Of course – I'll survive.*

*Must survive.*

*I am surviving right now.*

*Despite the army of crabs sizing me up.*

*I cut into their ranks a little.*

*Ha!*

*It's war!*

*But I'll be asked how Fred died, I mean.*

*They will ask that.*

*I meant to get back to that, but I was thinking of war with the crabs.*

*They will ask – about Fred, that is.*

*Not the crabs, I mean.*

*Who will ask?*

*Everyone.*

*The world, I imagine.*

*Fred's family.*

*All of it out there past that rusting wreck that never moves.*

*Only the waves move.*

*They crash around it.*

*Well, he died.*

*He died.*

*Just died.*

*Didn't wake up.*

*Made no sound.*

*Just died.*

*That's not how I would tell his family.*

*I will tell his family.*

*But that's how it was.*

*He just didn't wake up one day.*

*What day?*

*No – I won't calculate that.*

*I won't calculate my coming birthday, either.*

*I'll look forward to celebrating it on Howland.*

*Or even Honolulu.*

*With George.*

*With anyone.*

*Anyone would be welcome*

*And anywhere but Crab Island.*

*No – Fred Noonan Island.*

*So, I buried Fred in the sand.*

*A Herculean task.*

*I used chunks of broken glass and pieces of wood.*

*To dig, I mean.*

*And much energy in the heat.*

*Thank God some water had collected in shells.*

*Did I mention that water is gold?*

*Gold would mean nothing here.*

*But I repeat myself.*

*I wish Fred were still here to tell me I repeat myself.*

*But Fred is dead.*

*That's merciful, perhaps.*

*We'll see.*

*I'm not convinced yet.*

*After the burial I said a prayer.*

*For both of us.*

*Tears streaked my cheeks – valuable moisture.*

*From the corner of an eye I saw a crab at a distance, spying on me.*

*I sit on the beach.*

*At water's edge.*

*The night is calm.*

*Stars shimmer, never end.*

*The moon is my companion.*

*I sit with knees tucked under my chin.*

*Hands on my knees.*

*Gazing out into the black night.*

*Into the mass of ocean.*

*My mind plays tricks.*

*I think I see ship lights.*

*But nothing is there.*

*I have to remind myself of that.*

*No Itasca to the rescue.*

*But it doesn't have to be Itasca.*

*Any ship will do.*

*Drop anchor and come get me.*

*I'll swim out to you.*

*Climb aboard.*

*My quarters can be cramped, dirty.*

*The food in your galley without taste.*

*As long as you don't serve crabs.*

*The surf falls on the beach.*

*A pleasant sound.*

*It could reassure, soothe, comfort.*

*If the stakes weren't so high.*

*This place could be paradise.*

*If it weren't hell.*

*Think of it:*

*Over there – a hotel.*

*A restaurant or two.*

*Lifeguards sitting high in those chairs.*

*With that white stuff on their noses.*

*It's really a lovely beach.*

*A place to read a book.*

*From the beach I imagine my gaze can reach all the way to America.*

*And I can see the glow of lights on a coast.*

*A city!*

*What city?*

*San Francisco, I think.*

*A grand place, San Francisco.*

*I expel a sigh, slowly.*

*And close my eyes.*

*My hands reach ahead of me – And I'm flying again!*

*Oh, God!*

*Exquisite!*

*Wondrous!*

*My hands grip the steering column.*

*The engines drone loudly, wonderfully.*

*The propeller blades cut into the air, and my beloved Electra is whole again.*

*She soars!*

*I soar!*

*I touch gauges and the glass windshield*

*I glance over my shoulder.*

*There is an airplane all around me, enveloping me, supporting me, holding me.*

*All is real.*

*All is well.*

*All is all is all is all.*

## The Girl in Brown Who Walks Alone

*I close my eyes and off I go again into the glorious past:*

The next Sunday arrives and that morning I debate whether to go downtown and meet Ernest. I have not told Mother about him, even though I feel it is an innocent friendship. In those Chicago days I had not been good at all at making friends and really I had none at Hyde Park High. In my yearbook it says I am the girl in brown who walks alone. Did I really wear so much brown? I think on it and realize there is much truth to that. I dresse as I dressed, though, and I was satisfied with it.

But it's true I was often alone. But not always lonely. I attended classes and cared for Mother and so I suppose the image of me as a solitary brown figure has credibility. It's even a bit romantic, though I certainly didn't cultivate such things. Still, I recognized the value of a friend here and there and so, on a blustery day, I make the long walk to Michigan Avenue after all.

As I walk down the avenue to the diner I have mixed feelings, yet it would be fun to see Ernest. I do like him, and enjoyed him. It is like basking in the eccentric glow of someone rather electric. But, on the other hand, if he fails to show up, I would not be crestfallen. He is, after all, only slightly more than a stranger, no matter how luminous he could be. And I had become used to my solitary ways and my goal of finishing high school so I could move on. Bryn Mawr is still on my mind. I suspect I would try and go there. A glorious next step in life. But a friend is a glorious thing, too, and especially one like Ernest, who has an imagination and is not dull. Like me, he looks toward the future, not content to stay in place.

The sun is peeking from behind light clouds and the air was cool but not cold. The wind is deflected somewhat once I reach downtown and the shelter of tall buildings, denying the wind full reign to thoroughly scour the city. Still the breeze has strength and could suddenly whip around a corner in from the lake and down a street and pop off the hat of a lady who has not secured it adequately. I saw it happen once.

I walk at a brisk pace and enjoy the exercise. Many people are on the street, and I enjoy the random snatches of conversation and the many different types of clothing and hats, the men standing in clumps smoking cigars and chattering with easy smiles. A sudden swoosh of wind topples the cap from one man's head and his compatriots laugh as they watch him chase down the street after it. I too laugh as the hat cartwheels as though it has a life of its own.

On up ahead, as I navigate my way through throngs of people, is the diner. Ernest stands just outside the door, hands in the pockets of his dark jacket as he looks out at the street. He seems lost in thought. Perhaps his fertile imagination is concocting new stories to regale friends with. He glances my way and sees me, and there is the magnificent grin I had first seen the previous Sunday. It was worth the walk to experience that grin again. He slips off his cap as I approach. As the breeze scrubs his hair, dark strands fall on his forehead, which accentuated the notion of Ernest as likeably unkempt.

"But why do you wait on the street, Ernest? I would have found you inside."

"That wouldn't do," he says. "This way we can go in together. More proper."

"I see. Being the proper gentleman, are you, Ernest?"

"Hemingstein."

I laugh softly.

"We'll start off with Hem, and then see about this Hemingstein business."

"Deal." He opens the door for me and even bows slightly.

Inside it's warm and crowded as usual and loud, but in a comforting, social manner. There are several empty stools at the counter by the door, and I drift toward them, but Ernest steers me to a booth, the only one available as several people get up to leave, and we slide in and are quite snug in the comfort of padded seats and a good vantage point from which to survey the room. Ernest appears quite satisfied with the choice and I sense that he likes being where he can keep an eye on all that swirls about him.

"Stools wouldn't be right for old pals," Ernest says. "A booth is just right."

"Now we're old pals, Hem?"

"Sure we are. Thick as thieves."

That grin, on cue.

"We're thieves are we now?" I say.

"We are," he says confidently. "We're stealing the moment and living."

"I thought we were having lunch."

"That, too!"

He rolls his shoulders and winces slightly. Then he absently rubs one of them for a moment.

"Are you okay, Hem?"

"Sore shoulder," he says, rubbing it some more.

"Did you walk into a door?" I say, chuckling.

The grin spreads.

"Naw—I ran into the other team. Football. Yesterday at Phipps Field."

"Ah," I say. "You play for your school, is that it?"

"I'm on the second team – but next year, I'll be on the first team. I'll be bigger then."

"Did you win yesterday?" I ask.

"We did."

He looks quite proud.

"Football's a tough sport, Hem."

"That's what makes it great," he says. "It builds character."

"And bashes shoulders," I say.

He nods, but keeps the grin, and rubs his shoulder again.

"War wounds," he says and I suspect he sees the game as more than a game.

The waitress arrives and Ernest orders ham steak and au gratin potatoes and I order the same. Long walks make me very hungry.

"Will it snow soon?" I say as we wait for our orders.

"Naw," Ernest says. "Plenty of time before that."

"The fall here is pleasant."

"It's a swell place, Chicago," he says. "Do you like it?"

"I'm enjoying it, yes. I keep busy. But my trips downtown are fun."

"When it does snow," he says, "you'll take shorter walks, I guess."

"Perhaps. But I'll get out just the same."

"That's the spirit," Ernest says. "How's your mother?"

"Doing better, thanks. Tell me about *your* mother."

He glances away, toward the counter and people huddled on stools in a row, reminiscent to me of birds huddled along a branch.

"Not much to tell," he says with a shrug. "She sang once at Carnegie Hall, in New York."

"Really? How exciting. She's a singer?"

"Before she met my father." He shrugs again and glances absently toward the counter and the backs of people. "Not now. She gives lessons though. And plays a small concert here and there."

"I see. And you have brothers and sisters?"

"Four sisters."

"Goodness—you are surrounded by women, Hem!"

"I guess I am!" he abruptly gushes, and then the food arrives and we are both quite hungry. We don't speak for a minute as we both enjoy the ham and potatoes. The ham has a touch of honey to it and is tender and delicious. Ernest happily shovels his food into his mouth and his face expresses the pleasure of eating.

After eating, Ernest eases back in the booth, satisfied. He looks around the diner, his eyes seeming to catch every movement, his ears every word and sound. To some I imagine he seems merely playfully self-centered, but I suspect he is very aware of everything around him and misses little. And he's the sort of boy who can make friends anywhere. A part of me envies that skill. And a part of me knows I can stand being alone when that is the path I am on. Chicago is a pleasant and temporary stop in my journey. But that is surely true for Ernest, too.

"We should have some pie," Ernest announces suddenly and he motions the waitress to come by.

"Dare we?" I say. "After the lovely ham and potatoes?"

"Live a little, Amelia."

"But I do, Hem. I live very well, I think."

"There's always room for more," Ernest says, tacking on the grin.

We eat slices of blueberry pie, the waitress claiming the blueberries came from Michigan far across the lake.

"Michigan blueberries," Ernest says, his mouth full. "The best."

"I'll take your word as my guide to all things Michigan, Hem."

"Can't you call me Hemingstein just once?"

What is it about these nicknames, I think. Certainly they're endearing. But he relishes them so. Why is that?

"Okay," I say. "Hemingstein."

He beams brightly and his face threatens to disappear into the grin. He seems to have an obsessive need to label all around him as he sees fit. And he obviously needs the nicknames for himself to express the many sides that comprise him. So much energy bubbling inside a boy not even out of high school. He must have an ever replenishing spring inside him. I see how we are the same, a kindred spirit and unexpectedly so. Is this what draws me to Ernest? We walk different paths but toward the same horizon.

"How old are you, Hem?" I realize immediately I'm rather blunt in asking. But I have always been a bit outspoken.

He seems unperturbed.

"Fifteen," he says, wiping his hands on his napkin. "But going on sixteen."

"I'm older than you, Ernest."

"Hemingstein."

"I'm older than you—Hemingstein."

"A little, I guess," he says.

"And I finish school after the winter, Hemingstein. You have much more to do."

"Not so much," he says. "It goes fast."

"And I will surely leave Chicago then, Hemingstein. Even though it's quite pleasant."

"And so we're friends now," he says. "No matter what the future brings."

"Yes — friends." I smile and know there's no more to say on the subject. I like Ernest. It's difficult *not* to like such a boy.

The lunch crowd begins to empty out of the diner and Ernest offers to walk with me a bit.

"More of being the proper man, Hemingstein?"

His grin this time is more sheepish than magnificent.

"Good manners," he says.

After walking a while, we stop on a bridge over the Chicago River, populated with boats of various sizes. The wind has finally meandered off somewhere else, and the sun is mild and so pleasant.

"Does the river remind you of Michigan?" I say.

"A little." He looks down at the water a moment. "But it can't compare to Walloon Lake. Or the rivers we fish up there."

"What's the name again of your little town up there?"

"Petoskey."

"And it's on Lake Michigan?"

"Yes—on Little Traverse Bay."

"And your Walloon Lake is where?"

"Just south of Petoskey."

"It all sounds so lovely."

"It's grand, alright," he says. "Tell me about the Missouri River."

"It's a rather plodding, brown mass of water."

"Like the Mississippi, I suppose," he says.

"Not as big—but there once were riverboats at Atchison."

"That would be grand," he says. "Floating a long and slow river on a riverboat. Like Huck Finn and Tom Sawyer."

"I can see you doing that—Hemingstein."

"I just might." The grin makes an appearance.

"And it would not surprise me," I say. "Well, I must start the trek back to Hyde Park."

"So soon?"

"I told Mother I would be back at a certain time to help with dinner."

"The walk will make you ready for dinner," he says.

"It always does." I glance south, the direction home.

"Amelia—would you like to go on a picnic with me?"

"Now?"

"No—next Sunday. On the lake."

"Will the weather hold?"

He shrugs. "If it doesn't, we can always eat indoors."

"I don't know, Ernest."

"Meet me at the diner," he says. "But late morning. I'll get us a lunch to take, and we can walk to the lake. It's not far."

He's so enthusiastic that I hear myself agreeing to meet him at ten o'clock the next Sunday. I do fancy exploring the lakeshore.

"Knowing you is a lot of exercise, Hemingstein."

"It's healthy, too. Friends make you live long."

"I don't doubt it. Well—Sunday, then." I turn and head south and stop after a few steps. "Hemingstein—how do you get home each Sunday?"

"I have my ways." He waves and I wave, too, and then head home. I look back once more, from a distance, and he is still on the bridge, looking out over the water. I can imagine his grin.

## The Canary

*I wake up. The island is still there. I'm still on it.*

*I start a conversation with Fred.*

*Until my eyes focus and I remember Fred is dead.*

*He sleeps now under the sand.*

*Over there.*

*A short walk.*

*In the shade of a tree.*

*Poor man.*

*But safe from the crabs.*

*I must remember to tell his family he was brave.*

*And comforting.*

*We told jokes.*

*Until we ran out of jokes.*

*I wonder what George is doing now.*

*Looking for me.*

*How?*

*He will figure that out.*

*I can't help him with that.*

*He will know what to do.*

*A resourceful man.*

*The good husband.*

*Meanwhile, I am here.*

*Where else would I be?*

*I do my part.*

*By being ready to be rescued.*

*I prowl the beach.*

*And practice waving my arms.*

*It's all I can do.*

*But if the planes come back it will be enough.*

*I will be ready.*

*And I will laugh at the crabs.*

*I sit against the trunk of a palm on the edge of the beach.*

*A view of the ocean.*

*Lookout duty.*

*Must be vigilant.*

*I watch for ships.*

*And listen for planes.*

*And the crabs.*

*But they are elsewhere for now.*

*Doing whatever crabs do.*

*Plotting.*

*But for now, a truce in our war.*

*I called her The Canary.*

*She was a yellow Kinner Airster.*

*A biplane.*

*Quite small.*

*My first airplane.*

*I was so proud!*

*Not a sparkling new airplane mind you.*

*A little two-seater.*

*A tad underpowered.*

*Quite unreliable, really.*

*Neta Snook, my flying teacher, had advised against it.*

*She was unsure of me, too.*

*Perhaps she had more confidence in The Canary than in me – at first.*

*But I would not be deterred.*

*I had to fly.*

*It was not so long ago, really – 1921.*

*Though, now, yes, it seems a while.*

*But The Canary became mine and we became one.*

*And I set a record with it – a woman's record, so they termed it.*

*A record is a record.*

*As if the air at fourteen-thousand feet is somehow different for a woman than it is for a man.*

*I wake abruptly,*

*The Canary still an image in my brain for a moment.*

*Then it dissolves into nothing.*

*Come back!*

*Perhaps it will.*

*I will make it so.*

*Later.*

*For now, I am awake.*

*I focus my eyes.*

*A solitary crab sits in the shade of a palm not far away.*

*It watches me.*

*A scout.*

*Sent ahead by the others.*

*They know what they're doing.*

*The devils.*

*More plotting.*

*More intrigue.*

*I move toward it.*

*It scurries away.*

*To make its report.*

*I sit down again and quickly nod off.*

*When I wake again the first thing on my mind is the day we landed here.*

*The "crash."*

*But I suppose it's not so much of a crash if we walked away – limped away.*

*This was not my first crash.*

*Was it a crash?*

*A forced landing.*

*Hard landing.*

*We had no choice.*

*Ran out of gas.*

*But we made the reef.*

*No one killed – a good landing.*

*The damage – irrelevant.*

*No gas left anyway.*

*Call it a crash, if people will.*

*Fine with me.*

*I should ask the crabs how they view it.*

*There were other crashes.*

*One was trifling: a hard landing in Cora Kinner's cabbage patch.*

*I smile at the memory of cabbage stuck in wheels and propeller.*

*Another time:*

*With Neta.*

*In the Airster – The Canary.*

*The Canary stalled.*

*But not its fault – mine.*

*I clipped eucalyptus trees.*

*And made a mess of it.*

*Broke the propeller.*

*And undercarriage.*

*I cut my chin!*

*But I remembered to cut the engine.*

*And when Neta climbed out to look at me.*

*I was powdering my nose.*

*I smiled:*

*"We must look good for the reporters!"*

# Picnic

*I fall into the past:*

It occurred to me that I should prepare something to take to meet Ernest on Sunday. Nothing grand, but an offering. After all, he was to be my tour guide of the lakeshore. Never much of a cook, I made a passable potato salad and mother donates several slices of apple pie—Ernest seems to love his pie!

I hesitated to tell Mother about Ernest. But I didn't care to pretend that my Sunday explorations were uneventful and solitary. She thought it a fine idea to have a boy for a friend and she was kind enough not to pry and make too much out of it. She had been frankly concerned by my lack of social activities at school. A lonely, solitary girl needed people, she had mentioned several times, and I assured her I was not lonely and that solitary was something that depended on circumstances and could be withstood. As for people, I didn't need so many. She wanted to know if Ernest was handsome, and I confessed that he was quite handsome, but just a friend. And still a boy. A good companion. Someone with a zest for living who was fun to know. And he knew his way around Chicago. Mother seemed to accept that.

It is cooler on this Sunday, but still comfortable enough in my wool coat and hat, and I am quite used to being outdoors where walking helps keep me warm. I crave the exercise because of so much time spent sitting with Mother. There is no wind and I hope that to be true at the lakeshore as well. A smattering of clouds looks like they could only delay the sun's appearance until we reach Lake Michigan. I am so hoping for clear weather so I can properly assess the lake and shoreline.

I am right on time and Ernest is waiting outside the diner. He holds up a bag: "Lemonade and ham and cheese sandwiches!" he said enthusiastically.

I hold up my bag:

"And potato salad and apple pie!"

Ernest arches his eyebrows.

"A feast!"

"And good weather, Hem. A nice omen for our picnic."

It is not far to the lakeshore. We walk farther north on Michigan Avenue and then over to Lake Shore Drive—and there is the lake—the Midwest ocean. Motor cars and horse-drawn buggies crawl along the road and people stroll happily along the walkways. Many trees stand beyond the road along the sandy beach. No breeze stir and now the sun is out, the lake itself calm, the waves small, as they land on the beach. I shield my eyes and look out over the blue water and see a ship, puffs of black smoke erupting from its stacks.

"It's glorious, Ernest." I glance at him and he's looking out over the water, too, smiling. He has pushed his cap back on his head for a better look.

"You should see the shore from way out there," he says, pointing out into the lake. "We take a lake steamer from here to Petoskey."

"Is it far?"

"Yes." He points not across the lake, but north. "Petoskey is way up north. The trip takes more than thirty hours."

"Is that Michigan or Indiana straight across, Hem?"

"Michigan. Indiana is just to the south, though."

"It's all much grander than the Missouri River," I say, looking up into his eyes. "Come, let's go down to the beach."

We walk for a time along the beach and I wish it were warm enough to kick off shoes and dampen feet in the surf. Soon we are hungry, and retreat to the base of a large oak just across Lake Shore Drive where we dig into our lunch. The ham and cheese sandwiches buttressed by potato salad and apple pie prove to be quite enough, even for someone who enjoys eating as much as Ernest.

"Did your mother make the sandwiches, Hem? Or did you?"

"I made them. Are they okay?"

"Delicious."

"Did you make the pie?" he says.

I shake my head. "Mother made it. But I made the potato salad."

"I could live on potato salad," he says with a mouthful of it.

"And pie?"

"And pie, too," he says.

After lunch we lean against the trunk of the tree and gaze out at the lake. I could watch the waves forever.

"What do you do all summer in Petoskey?" I ask.

"Fish. Swim. Eat." He grins.

"A paradise, Hemingstein."

"I can't complain."

After a minute or two I say, "What do you think of the war, Hem?"

"I don't know," he says. "Maybe the British and French will end it soon. But I guess the Germans mean business."

"I'm sure they do," I say. "But I fear it won't be a short affair."

He shrugs. "Short or long—I guess it doesn't really affect us."

"It could, though," I say. "It very well might."

"You think we'll get in it?" He frowns.

"I think wars spread, Hem. And once started—hard to stop."

He looks out at the lake a moment.

"Maybe that's what it'll take," he says. "Us getting in. Maybe I'll have to go."

"You should hope not, Hem. And you're too young."

"Now I am," he says. "But if it lasts, who knows."

"Then I pray it ends soon."

He shrugs again, grins.

"We'll see. It still seems kind of remote. My father says it's European business."

I nod, but Ernest is looking out at the lake again.

"When will the cold weather come, Hem?"

"Not today. Probably not tomorrow. But soon enough. Sometimes, though, snow waits until almost December."

"Plenty of time," I say. "And October seems to be a good month in Chicago."

"Unless it snows tomorrow," he says, grinning. "You never know."

I look up at the sky, imagining I might see white flakes begin to fall, but the sky is azure blue and looks quite friendly.

"And so how is school, Hem?"

"Good. Yours?"

"It's school, Hem. Something to finish and then move on. After the coming winter, it will be almost done."

"Then college?"

"Yes. Bryn Mawr, I hope. We'll see. You have much more high school ahead of you, Mr. Hemingstein."

"A couple years, I guess," he says, unconcerned. "I want to play football again next year."

"Football's a rough sport."

"That's what makes it great."

"Are you big enough?" I say.

"I will be then. I'm sure of it. I grew more this year. I will next year, too."

"Keep eating those ham and cheese sandwiches."

"And pie," he says.

Now it's my time to grin. I look up, at the tree, and watch for a moment as a gentle breeze scrubs the branches.

"Shall we start back?" I say. "I promised Mother I would help with some things."

"Sure. But did you like the lake?"

"I love the lake. It's grand. It's even more than I expected, Hem."

"Good." He smiles, quite satisfied that he fulfilled a duty. He certainly likes to share his wonderment about something, about a place, with others. He is a perpetual sun needing orbiting planets.

In front of the diner on Michigan Avenue we say our goodbyes. A man hurrying past accidentally brushes my shoulder with his and I notice Ernest bristling—a momentary flash of emotion. Anger?

"I'm glad you came, Amelia," he says after a moment.

"Me, too. You showed me the lake. I'm grateful—and for lunch, too."

"Are you up for more adventure, Amelia?"

Such a persistent boy. Always looking for something to see or do. I confess that it can be contagious, though I don't want to encourage Ernest to believe we are somehow romantic instead of friends.

"What sort of adventure do you mean, Hem?"

"Next Saturday," he says. "The new Weeghman Park. North of here a bit. It's a new baseball field, just built. Want to go?"

"For a game?"

"Not a regular game—a special exhibition. The team is called The Chicago Federals—they played their first season earlier in the year."

"So, this wouldn't be a real game, Hem?"

"It's a real game, but not a season game. The season starts in April. This game is to keep people interested until then."

"I see. And they call themselves the Federals?"

"Yeah—I think it sounds funny, too. But they need a name. It's no worse than Chicago Cubs, I guess. It's their first season."

"The Cubs?"

"No—the Federals. It's the Federal League—a new league."

"So the team and league have the same name. Isn't that confusing, Hem?"

"You'll get the hang of it," he says.

"And where do the Cubs play?"

"West Side Grounds," he says. "And the Sox play at Comiskey."

"How does one keep track of it all?"

"People have their teams," he says.

"And which one is yours?"

"The Cubs, I guess."

"But we'd be going to the Federals?"

He shrugs and grins.

"Baseball is baseball."

"If you say so, Hem."

"It's supposed to be a swell park," he says, "with covered bleachers in case it rains."

His enthusiasm for anything and everything is always compelling, I realize, and I can't quite resist more fun with my only friend in Chicago.

"Okay," I say. "I'll give it a try."

"Meet here, at the diner," Ernest says. "There's food at the ballpark, I think."

"Should I bring something, just in case?" I say.

"Naw. There are places near the park, too."

"Saturday, then," I say. "Till then, Hemingstein."

"I'm going to work on a nickname for you, Amelia."

"Be kind," I say, but I know he will choose something affectionate.

I smile and he does, too, and then I turn and walk south on Michigan Avenue. I don't look back this time because I know Ernest is still standing there, his grin spreading.

## Once There Were Wings

*Inevitably I must roll out of the stupor and face the island yet another day.*

*I think about what was – flying. What can I say about flying?*

*It was a revelation.*

*The blood of my life.*

*Life itself.*

*Like drinking water.*

*Just as essential.*

*But it took effort.*

*I caught a streetcar to get to Kinner Field for lessons with Neta.*

*But the end of the streetcar line left me three miles short.*

*I walked the rest of it every time.*

*For two years.*

*I believe I established commitment, perseverance, desire.*

*Though Neta said my bad habit was to hold the Canuck's nose too high.*

*It would not take so long to walk around this island.*

*A long tight circle of a walk.*

*Though the crabs might object, of course.*

*Even try to stop me.*

*Where are they today?*

*Hatching plots, as usual.*

*I sit, think, remember:*

*Once I drove my mother from California to Boston.*

*In my 1923 Kissel Speedster.*

*Model 45 – called the "Goldbug."*

*Like The Canary, it was bright yellow.*

*Six-cycle.*

*Forty-one horsepower.*

*But I called it Yellow Peril.*

*That was 1924.*

*And we didn't go straight to Boston.*

*First, we drove north.*

*All the way to Canada.*

*Then east across Canada.*

*Six weeks of driving.*

*Adventurous.*

*In small towns we were an odd sight.*

*People turned out to see us.*

*I told Fred this story the day before he died.*

*It delighted him, I think.*

*Me, too.*

*On the beach, with a view of the grounded steamer, I visit the glorious past:*

It was such a long trip to Boston and we saw many amazing places and yet it was the first leg, to Yosemite, that comes to me immediately. Mother wanted to stop and prowl. I confess that I did, too. We found a lovely waterfall and a rainbow clung to it. A sign, my mother said, that our trip would be full of excitement and wonder.

We ate our lunch there, by the waterfall. When mother asked if I missed flying, I said that I did, of course, but that driving fulfilled my need for movement and adventure pretty well. Not nearly as well, of course, but very well indeed. And I would be in the air again soon enough. In the air or on the road—I felt a strong sense of freedom.

"And do you like being famous?" she asked as we finished lunch.

"*Am* I famous?"

"It would seem so, dear," she said.

"Why am I famous?"

"You are a woman who flies. "

"Is that so inconceivable?" I said.

"But you know the answer, Meelie."

"Do I? Is it really so odd, a woman flying?"

"To many people—yes, it does seem a little inconceivable."

"It should not." I said. "Does it to you?"

"Not anymore." She smiled sweetly.

I fear I will never see that smile again.

I hold it tight in my head.

*It finally rained.*

*Thank God.*

*I live some more.*

*Dark clouds had brewed and brooded over the ocean for some time.*

*Lightning flashed.*

*How far off?*

*I don't know.*

*It matters little.*

*Things are simply what they are.*

*When the rain came I sat in it, on the beach.*

*It soaked my clothes and skin.*

*I urged it to sink into me.*

*To make me a human ocean.*

*A sea.*

*A human swimming pool.*

*I wanted it to make me float on the sand.*

*I opened my mouth and let it fill me.*

*And remembered to set out open shells.*

*I watched them fill.*

*One drop at a time.*

*I could see the individual drops.*

*I'm sure of it.*

*Really.*

*My focus was that tight.*

*And then I wondered:*

*What do the crabs think of rain?*

*I have a comb.*

*I'd forgotten about it.*

*Humidity has made a mess of my hair.*

*It falls, limply.*

*Rather sadly.*

*Least of my worries, I know.*

*It has grown the past few weeks.*

*My hair, that is.*

*I can feel the new length.*

*I run the comb through my soggy hair.*

*The comb sails through the strands easily.*

*It feels good to comb my hair.*

*But I'm glad I don't have a mirror.*

## Fame

*I come back from the delusions.*
*Still on the island.*
*Where else would I be?*
*But I have accepted that.*
*Not really.*
*But I must maintain the charade.*
*Such fun to remember Ernest.*
*He was a charming boy.*
*I resolve to remember him again.*
*Very soon.*
*Welcome respite.*
*For those were innocent times.*
*With the future ahead of us.*
*Unknown.*
*In a wonderfully alive city.*
*Ernest grew into someone special after all.*
*Just as I expected.*
*Maybe not so startling after all.*
*There was something larger than life about him.*

*Even then.*

*In a Chicago diner.*

*A boy hurrying to become a man.*

*With a sense of destiny.*

*I read several of his intriguing books.*

*He became more than just a magnificent grin.*

*And I wonder now where he is.*

*What he's doing.*

*More books to write.*

*Over the years I would hear about him.*

*His destiny took brilliant turns.*

*But we both went far.*

*Far, far, far from that diner on Michigan Avenue.*

*We followed our destinies.*

*Were pulled along by our destinies.*

*I was grounded by my destiny.*

*Here.*

*I imagine his magnificent grin one more time.*

*I savor it a moment.*

*Then rise and walk down the beach.*

*I must know what the crabs are up to.*

*Water is an issue again.*

*None yet today.*

*Last night I had some from open shells.*

*Not enough.*

*I go inland.*

*And search trees.*

*Finally I am lucky.*

*Water collected in the crook of a tree.*

*It brings me back.*

*Back for what?*

*Back to keep going.*

*To keep hoping.*

*I keep myself ready.*

*Surely someone will yet come.*

*They have not forgotten me.*

*I must believe that.*

*If only it would rain more.*

*I could do a little rain dance.*

*But I must conserve energy when I can.*

*To be ready should help arrive.*

*And to deal with the crabs.*

*This morning they sent a solitary scout to spy on me.*

*It appeared here and there.*

*On a low sand rise.*

*From behind trees.*

*Scurrying about.*

*But at a distance.*

*And always watching.*

*It watches, records.*

*Making notes, I imagine.*

*Remembers.*

*I fear a new phase in the crab war.*

*Last night an attack in some force.*

*Sudden.*

*Well-planned.*

*Rehearsed, perhaps.*

*It left me bloodied.*

*A new tactic, perhaps.*

*Gone are the days of solitary scout crabs.*

*Keeping track of me is not enough.*

*Snip and run – not enough.*

*Gouge and slide away – not enough.*

*They want it all.*

*These devious crabs.*

*Greed.*

*While I slept a dozen made the rush.*

*My arm and leg bloodied.*

*I fought back.*

*But surprise is a good tactic.*

*I got two of them.*

*Saved myself.*

*And managed a breakfast.*

*Meat and moisture.*

*Like gold.*

*But far more useful.*

*I clean myself up.*

*Look around.*

*No scout crabs.*

*They're with the main force, no doubt.*

*The crab legion.*

*The crab army.*

*Celebrating the successful skirmish.*

*Plotting how to win the war.*

*I limp to the beach.*

*Ease into the ocean.*

*To let the salt scour my wounds.*

*I feel the salty sting.*

*And wince.*

*And have fleeting images.*

*Of walking the Lake Michigan shore with Ernest.*

## Baseball is Baseball

*And off I go to my beloved past:*

There was no food at Weeghman Park, and so Ernest bought roast beef sandwiches in a neighborhood store, and we washed them down with a bottle of milk. It was rather charming, and certainly filling, and some spicy mustard livened up the cold beef and tasteless bread. Ernest apologized profusely, but I assured him that we ate very well indeed. The weather held up nicely—no rain, the sun darting in and out of clouds, and in our wool coats the temperature was quite tolerable. When the sun was out, it bathed our foreheads and felt quite glorious. An intermittent breeze, Ernest explained, could affect the pitching of the ball. That science aspect I understood and that interested me.

The new field, I learned, was at Addison and Clark streets. A crowd swelled outside the gates when we arrived. Attendance was hard to judge—certainly thousands of people. A sea of men and women in all sorts of hats. Ernest relished being in the crowd and looked around eagerly, a smile on his face, and since we had arrived at the park early we secured excellent seats down close to the field, where we could really see the action. Ringing the park were some apartment buildings and we could see people perched on roofs to watch the game. A woman next to us exclaimed that the elevated train that morning had been crowded with people coming to the game. Before the game started some ladies displayed a very large American flag down on the field and Ernest said they were members of the Daughters of the Grand Army of the Republic.

"The Federals' manager, Joe Tinker, lives in Oak Park," Ernest proclaimed proudly. "Not so far from my house.

Before the game began, people all around us debate the war in Europe. I took it that many people knew men who wanted to go fight in it, which struck me as foolish because it was not an American war yet, though I reminded Ernest that I fear it would spread and we will be pulled into it. Two men behind us puffing on cigars are quite animated about the war, but they strike me as too old to fight. I am happy to see that Ernest doesn't seem interested in the war talk and is instead enjoying the sight of this new baseball field and the men in their uniforms jogging to and fro to warm up for the game. Ernest assures me that the Federals pitcher, Claude Hendrix, is a good one known for throwing something called a spitball.

"It doesn't sound very hygienic, Hem."

"But all the teams have guys who do it. It's practically a baseball institution."

"This is quite the colorful sport."

"It's swell, ain't it?"

"Oh, yes, indeed," I say. "And maybe we get to see Mr. Hendrix spitting on the ball."

"He'll be sort of coy about it," Ernest says.

"An admirable quality. I prefer coy spitters."

"You understand the spitball?" he says.

"Socially?" I say. "Or scientifically?"

Ernest grins, perhaps not sure what I mean.

"I understand the science of it, Hem. Moisture on the ball will alter its path. I take it that's highly desirable?"

"Oh, yeah," he says. "The idea is to make the ball jiggle around a bit to confuse the batter."

"Ah," I say. "Jiggling and spitting. The refinements of baseball."

"See—I told you you'd get the hang of it all."

"Perhaps Mr. Hendrix should instead carry some sort of small canteen or container with water," I say.

"I don't think that would be allowed," Ernest says.

"But spitting is okay?"

"Great, ain't it?"

"Marvelous," I say, smiling.

But the event was fun nonetheless because the crowd is so animated by the ebb and flow of the game. Ernest joined the cigar-smoking men behind us in calling the opposing pitcher a bum with no arm, which I took to mean he was not a spitballer, or not a very good spitballer. I confess that I did not see him do any spitting. Mr. Hendrix, though, would bring the glove and ball up to his mouth quite often. It was funny to think of thousands of people making their way to this place to cheer a man who spits. But I confess that at some point I was as one with the crowd, too! I even called the other pitcher a bum. But not Mr. Hendrix, of course!

After the game, people linger in the stands and socialize and smoke, and the war debate is revived among the people sitting near us. Ernest announces he is still hungry and I am, too, and so we slip out of the park ahead of the crowd and Ernest suggests a late lunch somewhere.

"Or maybe it's an early dinner," he adds.

"Shall we go back to the diner on Michigan?" I ask.

"Let's find another joint. And be adventurous."

"You be the guide, Hem."

"Do you like spaghetti?" he asks.

"I do. Where shall we go?"

"I know a swell Italian place on State Street."

"Is it far?"

"On your way home, practically. Are you tired?"

"Not at all. Walking is so bracing."

"It makes me hungry," he says.

We find the small restaurant tucked between two department stores. It's early for dinner and few people are eating. The waiter is quite comical with very dark, oiled hair parted down the middle and one of those outrageous handlebar mustaches and such a serious demeanor. Ernest nicknames him The Hairy One. The Hairy One brings us our plates of steaming spaghetti and sliced bread with butter and we dig in, and it's a proper meal. The spaghetti is heavenly, the sauce a little cheesy, and I like it. Ernest consumes all on his plate, wiping up the leftover sauce with bread and I follow suit. The best meal I have had in some time.

"So, Hem—what about this business of a nickname for me?"

"Did you have one growing up?"

"Meelie."

"That's good," he says. "I like it."

"But where's *your* version?" I say. "Has the great Hemingstein come up empty?"

"I could call you Tall Girl."

"Except that I'm a woman, Hem. Not a girl."

"Oh. I see."

"Do you?"

"Sure."

"Am I so tall, Hem?"

"You're almost as tall as me."

"But I think I've stopped growing," I say. "And you expect to grow this year, you said—to play football."

"Fingers crossed," he says.

"Or fingers broken, Hem. Football won't be like Mr. Hendrix tossing those spitballs."

"I'll be ready for it," he says, puffing himself up a bit, which was endearing.

After leaving the restaurant we make our way to Michigan Avenue and toward the bridge over the river, our usual point of goodbye.

"You never mention school, Amelia."

"There's nothing to mention. It's a job, sort of. Something to finish so I can move on."

"Maybe I'll feel the same way in a year or so," he says.

"Enjoy your time there, Hem. You have friends and activities and you're young. Relish the experience."

"But you don't."

"It's different for me," I say. "We just moved here and at the end of the school year I'll move again. And I'm used to moving, I suppose."

We reach the bridge and look down at the Chicago River. I know I have to get going soon, as there is not much light left.

"Hem, would you like to visit Hyde Park next week?"

His face brightens and the magnificent grin returns.

"Sure I would," he says.

I feel obligated to be his host after all his goodwill and good company. And I like him well enough to offer.

"We could go to the lake again," I say. "There may not be many more opportunities for that, I suspect."

"Should I bring food?" he asks.

No doubt he wants a chance to make up for the roast beef sandwiches. Such an eager gentleman.

"We can eat somewhere in my neighborhood," I say. "Do you think the weather will still hold?"

"It should," he says. "It'll be fine. There's still plenty of leaves on the trees."

"Is that a scientific observation, Hem?"

"Just a feeling. Believe me, there's plenty of fall left yet."

"Then we'll make the most of it," I say. "Do you know Washington Park, Hem? We could meet at the Rustic Bridge—I think you'd like it very much. It's made of logs and such. And people canoe the stream."

"I'll find it," he says. "Maybe we can take out a canoe."

"Maybe," I say. "We'll see. Now I really have to go. Mother will worry."

I turn and walk south and look back once, as usual, to wave to him and he waves enthusiastically and then turns north back across the bridge.

# Shelter

*I need better shelter on this island.*
*My own fortress.*
*Something safer from the Crab War.*
*But there is no escape from it.*
*They hatch their little plots.*
*And hatch new soldiers.*
*And plan their skirmishes.*
*Hold their rallies.*
*Cheer their leaders.*
*Compose their slogans.*
*Memorialize their fallen.*
*Erect their monuments.*
*Wave their banners.*
*While I keep moving.*
*Keep looking for water.*
*And food.*
*Their fallen sustain me.*
*Barely.*

*War with the crabs has escalated.*

*Inevitable, I suppose.*

*All their scouting missions, their plots, resulted in an attack.*

*While I was daydreaming.*

*About Neta, of course.*

*Wishing we could talk again.*

*Soon.*

*I suspect we will.*

*But as I luxuriated in the daydream, the attack was launched.*

*Sneaky:*

*Several crabs rushed from cover and bloodied me.*

*I woke with a shrill yelp.*

*Blood running down an arm.*

*I crushed both crabs with a stone.*

*They became my dinner.*

*Yet they were quite brave, I suppose.*

*I must give them that.*

*They sacrificed themselves.*

*For their cause.*

*I am their cause, of course.*

*But I will resist.*

*I won today's skirmish.*

*Ahead, on a slight rise of sand, a crab scout looks on.*

*It surveys the skirmish results, then scurries away.*

*To report back.*

*It will say that brave crabs died.*

*For their cause.*

*I have lost track of the days.*

*They all look the same.*

*Feel the same.*

*Smell the same*

*Start and end the same.*

*Is it my birthday yet?*

*No.*

*I think not.*

*Not yet.*

*Soon.*

*But that is still to come.*

*Will it come?*

*It must.*

*But will I know?*

*I think hard.*

*I concentrate.*

*And calculate the days*

*But I can't be sure.*

*And that worries me.*

*Though I conclude there's a way.*

*I shall go look for water.*

*Yes – motivation.*

*The moisture will revive me.*

*And my head will clear.*

*I will think.*

*Well enough, anyway, to decide how long it has been.*

*And when I will turn 40.*

*A birthday!*

*Having a plan refreshes me.*

*Having a plan is a comfort.*

*The crabs have plans.*

*Why can't I?*

*I go on a scouting mission of my own.*

*Impulsive, I know.*

*First, I scout the beach.*

*I stroll about, but there are no crabs.*

*Soon I cut into the island and emerge at the lagoon.*

*I am cautious, deliberate.*

*Peering from behind a palm tree trunk.*

*And soon I spot my quarry:*

*At a distance the crabs have gathered.*

*Many crabs.*

*A legion.*

*Banners fluttering in the wind.*

*Listening to their leaders giving speeches.*

*Whipping the legion into a frenzy.*

*A crab rally.*

*A crab call to arms.*

*And surely they all have heard of the day's earlier skirmish.*

*They will know I devoured their fallen comrades for dinner.*

*It will incense them.*

*Rally them.*

*I pull back from the tree trunk, to the beach.*

*It's clear of crabs.*

*I half expected one or two.*

*Perhaps fully expected one or two.*

*Because these crabs are clever.*

*I know they won't give up.*

*Neither will I.*

*I hope.*

*Later I napped.*

*But a sound woke me.*

*I looked around.*

*The crabs must be behind it.*

*Some byzantine plot on their part.*

*They scheme.*

*Out there, hidden in the foliage.*

*Or along the beach behind a rise.*

*Perhaps along the banks of the lagoon.*

*They're everywhere.*

*They work against me.*

*Building something, perhaps.*

*Machines of battle, I suppose.*

*There must be a crab workshop somewhere.*

*Below ground, perhaps – below sand.*

*Industrial crabs.*

*I am sure of it.*

*I look for their scouts.*

*But none appear.*

*They hide, I know.*

*Spy on me.*

*I look again for them on the beach.*

*But they are not there.*

*Interesting.*

*Puzzling.*

*A new form of crab deception, I suspect.*

*Diabolical.*

*Clever, these crabs.*

*I sit in the thin shade of a palm tree.*

*Gazing down the beach.*

*Soon a woman appears:*

*Neta!*

*It's Neta!*

*How wonderful to see her.*

*She waves.*

*Smiles.*

*Reaches me.*

*We hug.*

*Glorious.*

*She looks exactly like she did in 1921.*

*Still wears her flying leather.*

*Her hair – dark, curly.*

*Unkempt.*

*"But, dear," I say. "You are dressed too warmly for my island."*

*"Very true," she says. "But I'm fine. Don't fret over me."*

*"No, I won't," I say, smiling.*

*We hug again.*

*It's a delight to see her.*

*"I'm lonely, Neta."*

*"I know you are, dear."*

*She grips my hand.*

*Rubs it to soothe me.*

*"Fred is dead," I say.*

*"I know, dear," she says. "I know."*

*"I did my best," I say. "I tried my best."*

*"You always did," Neta says.*

*"It wasn't enough," I say. "I failed."*

*"No, dear," she says. "No one who truly tries can really claim failure."*

## The Rustic Bridge

*Off I go again, happily, into the peace of my past:*

I am standing on the little bridge made of logs, looking down into the stream, when Ernest arrives, his newsboy cap perched at a jaunty angle on his head, his hands buried in his coat pockets, but a cheery smile on his face. I wonder, do other people see and feel the glow that seems to radiate off this boy? As he gets closer, I see he limps slightly.

"This is a swell place," Ernest says as he reaches me and looks down into the water at our reflections.

"Rather like your Petoskey, Michigan?" I say.

He glances around at the trees, downstream at the flowing water. He rubs a hand along the coarse surface of the log railing. Two ducks pop around a bend, bobbing happily and chattering as they sail by.

"Yeah—it does kind of make me think of Michigan. But there's probably no trout in this stream."

"Are there many trout in Michigan?"

"All over the place," he says. "They jump into your pockets. When you turn a spigot, trout shoot out. They keep you company in the bathtub."

"Do they join you at dinner?"

"They *are* dinner," he says, laughing, and I laugh, too.

"You have a limp, I think, Hem. Did you hurt your leg?"

"Football, Meelie."

"That's right," I say. "I forgot—you play on Saturdays. Did you win?"

He nods and grins.

"Notch another one for the Great Hemingstein and his gallant boys."

I can imagine that in his head he is King Arthur and his teammates are his brave and loyal Round Table knights defending Camelot. The other boys might be playing football, but perhaps Ernest is fighting a war and leading his troops. Teammates see a football field and Ernest sees a field of battle with honor at stake.

"And your leg, Great Hemingstein—how did it come to be wounded?"

"Some oaf stepped on it."

"Ouch. Were you lying down on the job, so to speak?"

"Not willingly," he says, the grin more sheepish than magnificent.

"Well, at least you won."

"That's what matters," he says. "And the wounds are badges of honor."

No doubt he believes it.

"But it makes it hard to walk, Hem."

"It's not bad at all," he says. "I could go swimming right now, if it were warmer."

"Too chilly for that," I say and shake my head.

But the weather is actually quite pleasant. No breeze and the sun, though weak, is in and out from behind light fluffy clouds. We watch two laughing boys navigate a canoe under the bridge and head downstream. Awkward with the oars, they splash much water and the canoe drifts into a bank several times.

"They can't navigate," Ernest says. "They need to learn how to steer. It's crucial."

"But they are having great fun at it," I say. "I suppose canoes are standard fare up in your Michigan, Hem."

"Sure they are," he says emphatically. "Indians taught me how to steer. How to use the oars like an Indian. Now I'm practically an Indian myself."

I wonder how much of this is true. With Ernest perhaps it does not matter. He turns and goes to the other side of the bridge to examine the water upstream, his elbows on the railing as his eyes scan the water and stream banks. No doubt taking the measure of the stream, comparing it to his beloved Michigan streams. I also suspect that when he looks at something he sees more of it than other people. He sees all of something and understands how it works. That's how I am, too, I think, though I wonder if I am as good at it as Ernest. He seems born to absorb all around him and to retain it. I have to work at it a little harder.

"Shall we rest a bit?" I say. "It would do your leg good."

"All right," he says, and we leave the bridge for a spot on one of the banks with a good view downstream and a copse of trees behind us. The fall colors are brilliant—reds and oranges and yellows.

We sit and Ernest seems quite pleased to watch the water flow by and listen to it gurgle. In his head I suspect it's a stream of Michigan trout and he is planning where he will fish and how many he will catch and how triumphant he will be to present his catch to friends and family.

"Did you catch many?" I say after a bit.

He stares at me a moment, caught off guard.

"What do you mean?"

"Trout," I say. "I think you fish this stream in your head."

He nods and grins and slaps a thigh.

"Very good, Meelie. I confess."

"Did you catch many?"

"Not so many right here," he says. "But farther down, where the water deepens, I took many. Just like in Michigan."

"Lovely Michigan," I say. "You miss it."

"Always," he says. "But I just had my summer there. I'm good for the winter, I guess."

"And you have football."

"And big oafs stepping on my legs."

"And much to keep you occupied in school," I say. "What interests you, Hem?"

"Reading, I suppose. I've even tried some poetry."

"Really? I should like to see it. Maybe you're destined to be a poet."

"I don't know," he says. "Maybe. We'll see."

He shields his eyes with a hand and looks downstream with a long, penetrating gaze.

"When can I see your poems?" I say.

He glances away, upstream at the bridge.

"They aren't really poems yet, Meelie. Just lines here and there—thoughts. Notions. Fragments of poems. Starts of poems."

"Everything big starts off small, Hem."

"That's a good line," he says. "Maybe I'll steal it."

"My gift."

"What can I give in return?" he says.

"You already have," I say. "You have shown me so much of Chicago."

"Do you really like Chicago, Meelie?"

"Very much. It's grand."

"But it's not home for you," he says.

"No. It isn't. But a good place to finish school. It's *your* home, Ernest."

"Ernest?"

"Okay—Hemingstein."

"Better."

He lets the magnificent grin jump to life.

"You have Michigan in summer, Hem, but Chicago is your home, and it serves you well. Maybe you will become a famous Chicago poet."

He laughs, glances again downstream.

"I'm not a poet yet," he says. "And maybe not at all. Just a guy tossing a few words onto paper. Playing with words. Playing at poetry. And I can't say Chicago will always be home."

"No? Michigan, then?"

He shrugs.

"There's a big world out there, Meelie."

"Me, too," I say. "And soon. There's just the coming winter and then school here will be over. A new chapter starts."

"You'll go east," he says.

"I hope so."

"What will you be, Meelie? After college, I mean."

I think on it a moment and another canoe squirts from under the bridge. A handsome young man wearing a skimmer hat is paddling, and a pretty young lady sits in front, both hands gripping the sides of the canoe, but the man seems to know how to steer and handles his oar confidently, expertly, and without much splashing, the oar slipping in and out of the water with ease and the canoe flowing straight and down the center of the stream. Ernest notices, too.

"That's the way to do it," he says. "His stroke is good."

"Maybe he's an Indian," I say.

"He looks like a dude," Ernest says. "But he knows how to steer."

The canoe dashes past us, and we watch it a moment as it flows downstream, its course held steady in the center of the stream as it slices through the water.

"A real oarsman," Ernest says. "But he still looks like a dude."

"Is there hope, then, for dudes?" I say.

"Maybe so." He looks at me. "So, what did you decide—what do you want to be, Meelie?"

"Maybe I'll help people," I say. "Maybe college will help me decide how to do that. Or maybe the war will be a factor."

"The war? That's pretty far off, Meelie. A problem for Europe."

"For now it is, Hem. But maybe not for long."

"You think we'll eventually get in it?"

"I don't know," I say. "I just know wars don't just start and end the next day."

"I could go to England and volunteer," he says, but not convincingly.

"You're fifteen, Hem."

"I could pass for older. I'm growing all the time."

"And one day, in a war, you stop growing at all," I say.

"We'll see," he says. "I read about it in the papers. But it's hard to know how it's going. My grandfather fought in the Civil War. But he made it through."

"One of the lucky ones," I say. "There are always plenty of unlucky ones."

We sit quietly a while, just the sound of the flowing stream and a few chattering birds in the trees behind us.

"Should we go eat?" Ernest finally says.

"Brilliant idea, Hem."

He helps me up and we walk until we find a small, warm café near the University of Chicago. We sit in a cozy booth. It's not nearly as crowded or noisy as the diner we frequent on Michigan Avenue. Ernest is suddenly hungry for pancakes covered with maple syrup and also toast and butter with blueberry and strawberry jam. We both get stacks of pancakes and they prove delicious.

"You should come watch me play," he says after we eat.

"At one of your matches?" I say.

"Game, Meelie. Football's a game. Not a match."

"And do they allow spitballs, like Mr. Hendrix for the Federals?"

Ernest laughs.

"No—there's no spitballs. Though once I saw a guy spit on someone after a tackle."

"How disgusting," I say.

"That's what the guy thought, too," he says. "Only he didn't call it that. He used other words, if you know what I mean."

"Sports can be so odd, Hem. Spitting on a ball is okay in one sport and spitting on people happens in another."

"Well, it's not like spitting on someone is encouraged in football, Meelie. But football's more personal than baseball."

"How's your leg?" I say.

"Better all the time. Trivial, really."

"Stick to poetry, Hem. It's safer."

"But we need action in our lives to have something to write poems about."

"Are there any poems about spitting, Hem?"

"Maybe I could write one."

"No thanks," I say.

"A football poem, but with spitting in it," he says.

"I'm afraid not, Hem."

After we eat, I walk with Ernest back to the bridge so he can start his trek home.

"Come watch a game, Meelie."

"Where do you play again?"

"Phipps Field. It's at Chicago Avenue and Harlem."

"I have no idea where that is."

"I bet you can find it, though. You're practically a Chicagoan now."

"Am I?"

"Sure you are. Oak Park isn't so far from here. A matter of a few miles."

"I don't know, Hem. Will I have to watch players spitting?"

"Naw. That doesn't happen much."

"Will I have to watch you get hurt?"

"I promise—no injuries," he says.

"How can you promise that in so rough a sport?"

"Trust the Great Hemingstein."

He looks as hopeful as a puppy waiting for dinner.

"Maybe I can catch a ride out, Hem. But how do I get back?"

"If you can get there, I'll figure out how to get you home—trust me."

He has no idea how to do that, I realize, and yet I am sure he will figure it out. That's the sort of boy he is.

"No promises, Hem," I say, "but maybe I can manage it—we'll see."

He smiles grandly.

"Excellent. I'll look for you in the stands."

"If I'm there."

"You'll come, Meelie. It's an adventure. You're destined for adventure. It's in your bones."

"You're so sure?"

"Yeah, I am. We both are destined for adventure. I can feel it all through me."

"Maybe you're just catching a cold."

"I'll see you at the game," he says.

"Maybe you will, Hem."

He turns with a smile and strides off and I watch him a while. He does not seem to be limping anymore.

# Fred is Still Dead

*I stand over Fred's grave.*
*How long has he been dead?*
*I try not to think about time.*
*Would that help?*
*Probably not.*
*Poor Fred.*
*He didn't last long once we were down.*
*I wish I had his companionship.*
*And I wonder why I am lasting much longer.*
*Something inside me.*
*That's still strong.*
*Despite the hardships.*
*A will to live, I suppose.*
*Faith I will yet be rescued.*
*Hope a ship will yet appear on the horizon.*
*Have they forgotten me?*
*When I flew the world wanted to know me.*
*I drew crowds.*
*Have they forgotten Amelia?*

*I'm out of sight.*

*But am I out of mind?*

*I stare down at Fred's grave.*

*So sorry, old friend.*

*You died out of sight of the world.*

*I have cried for you.*

*I have cried for me.*

*Who do the crabs cry for?*

*Crabs do not cry.*

*Out of the corner of my eye I see two of them.*

*They slide slowly back into the cover of a tree line.*

*Spies.*

*Sentinels.*

*Something is afoot.*

*I can feel it.*

*The senses heighten.*

*When you are all alone.*

*Without thinking I start a conversation with Fred.*

*Until my eyes focus and I remember – Fred is dead.*

*Over there.*

*Just over there.*

*A short walk.*

*In the shade of a tree.*

*Poor man.*

*But safe from the crabs.*

*I must remember to tell his family he was brave.*

*And comforting.*

*We told jokes.*

*Until we ran out of jokes.*

*I wonder what George is doing now.*

*George. The good husband.*

*The good husband is looking for me.*

*How?*

*He will figure that out.*

*I can't help him with that.*

*But he will know what to do.*

*A resourceful man, the good husband.*

*Meanwhile, I am here.*

*Where else would I be?*

*I do my part.*

*By being ready to be rescued.*

*I prowl the beach.*

*And practice waving my arms.*

*It's all I can do.*

*But I will be ready.*

*And I will laugh at the crabs.*

*Later in the day I found water in open shells.*

*It revived me and I was honest with myself:*

*Neta had been a mirage.*

*I know that.*

*Now.*

*But she was a lovely, welcome mirage.*

*And perhaps I need the mirage.*

*To help cut the loneliness.*

*To keep my mind working, sharp.*

*I manage a meal of turtle and small birds.*

*It's not much.*

*But a lot, when seasoned with perspective.*

*After the meager meal, I sit at my lookout spot.*

*Overlooking the ocean.*

*Vigilant.*

*But tired.*

*And I think:*

*I didn't always want to fly.*

*I was eleven – no, perhaps ten – when I saw my first airplane.*

*At a fair.*

*It did not really impress me.*

*It was odd and rather annoying.*

*I ignored it.*

*Only years later did I realize I belonged up in the air, craved being in the air.*

*There's something about flying that's truly liberating.*

*One chooses a direction and off they go, unchained, and free of the earth.*

*Free of duties and obligations and politics – restrictions.*

*Flying = free.*

*For a woman, I think it's doubly so.*

*Neta understood that before just about anyone.*

*She handed me my freedom when she taught me to fly.*

*But I also seized the challenge.*

*I made myself.*

*And so what can I say about flying?*

*It was a revelation.*

*The blood of my life.*

*Life itself.*

*Like drinking water.*

*Just as essential.*

*But it took effort.*

*I caught a streetcar to get to Kinner Field for lessons with Neta.*

*But the end of the streetcar line left me three miles short.*

*I walked that shabby road every time.*

*For two years.*

*I believe I established commitment, perseverance, desire.*

*But Neta said my one bad habit was to hold the Canuck's nose too high.*

*I stayed in the past too long today.*

*Several crabs caught me napping.*

*Bloodied my leg.*

*But zeal was their mistake.*

*These two scurried far ahead of the squadron.*

*And bloodied me.*

*But woke me.*

*Alerted me.*

*Saved me, actually.*

*Ironic.*

*I escaped before the rest could settle the issue, perhaps.*

*Would that have been the end?*

*Maybe.*

*Maybe not.*

*I still have fight in me.*

*Plenty of fight.*

*But energy ebbs.*

*I go off, toward the lagoon.*

*I search for water.*

*The shells I left out are empty.*

*But I finally find water in a tree crook.*

*It's glorious, water.*

*Splendid.*

*More valuable than gold.*

*Gold would mean nothing here.*

*But perhaps I have mentioned that before.*

*I wish the crabs would pick a side of the island.*

*I would have the other side.*

*Just let me know.*

*Please.*

*We would co-exist.*

*Such a fantasy!*

*I eat them, when I can.*

*They attack me, when they can.*

*They resent me.*

*Can I blame them?*

*But don't they see?*

*I didn't choose this place, this island.*

*I was dropped from the sky.*

*An interloper on their island.*

*But I came from the sky!*

*They should view me as a God!*

*I could be their leader.*

*Except they have leaders.*

*I have seen them.*

*At crab rallies.*

*By the lagoon.*

*Why do they always rally at the lagoon?*

*I would choose the beach, the ocean.*

*It's a much better view.*

*Exactly like a postcard.*

*If I had a postcard, I would mail it.*

*But there is no post office.*

*Just crabs.*

*I slip into the tree line.*

*I look for water.*

*I find precious little.*

*But enough to sustain me some more.*

*I need food, too.*

*So I look for a solitary crab.*

*One that has strayed from the legions of crabs.*

*Will it be missed?*

*Of course.*

*Somehow they must know about every casualty.*

*Every battle loss.*

*And who is responsible.*

*Me.*

*The water is enough to clear my head.*

*I have been talking rot.*

*Making no sense.*

*I look for more water.*

*I must make sense.*

*Keep my sanity.*

## This is Where I Am Now

*No crabs in sight, so I drift effortlessly away, back to the lovely past:*

The weather was turning chillier, but it had not yet snowed, and it was still bearable to walk downtown. A little brisk at times, but bracing, and invigorating to me. All the walking I had done for months made me feel healthy and strong. The cool air made my cheeks glow.

I met Ernest at our old diner on Michigan Avenue. He stood outside, as usual, sort of rolling back and forth on the balls of his feet. He looked content. I always suspected that the clamor of the city and the people cruising past ignited his imagination. But a boy such as Ernest likely didn't need much spark to make the fire burn. The flame is always there inside him.

"Meelie," he says happily as he turns and spots me in the street crowd.

"Hemingstein," I call and he lumbers toward me smiling.

"It's cool and crisp today," he says. "Are you warm enough?"

"Perfectly fine," I say. "It's a bracing day. I love to walk."

"I'm hungry, Meelie. Let's eat."

"Of course you are, Hem. You always are."

Inside the diner it's warm and the front windows have fogged. Ernest helps me slip out of my wool coat, and he hangs our coats on a rack attached to the outside of our booth. Soon the waitress brings piping hot coffee and I warm my hands around the cup and feel the glow.

"What will you devour today, Hem?"

The sheepish look, elbowed away quickly by the grin.

"Do I eat so much, Meelie?"

"You're a growing boy, Hem. And a football player."

"We won again yesterday," he says proudly.

"And are you injured at all, Hem?"

"Naw. Not a bit. Like last time, I only saw a little action. It's tough to sit the bench."

"But do you learn as you sit, Hem?"

"I watch the other players," he says, nodding seriously. "I see how they do things."

"Next year, Hem. Hopefully next year is your year."

"Fingers crossed I grow some more," he says and when the waitress comes back to re-fill our coffee cups, he enthusiastically orders pancakes and toast with butter and jam. I had a good breakfast to start me off on my walk and I choose a ham and cheese sandwich.

"Will it snow soon, Hem?"

"Any day, maybe. Hard to say. But it's time, I guess."

"Not until I walk home, though," I say.

"You could walk fast to dodge the flakes, Meelie."

"I'm quite the walker, thanks to you, Hem."

He slides over toward the aisle for a moment and looks toward the door and windows.

"No snow," he says. "Our luck holds again."

"We *are* lucky," I say. "To be friends."

He nods, smiles, then frowns slightly.

"Have you made friends at school, Meelie? What about the boy you help with chemistry?"

"That was a transaction, Hem. I told you about that. Tutoring in exchange for a ride."

"But you sit next to him in class, Meelie."

"I pay attention in class," I say. "I have college ahead of me."

"Bryn Mawr," he says.

"I hope so, Hem. And you should go to college, too."

He shrugs his shoulders and then loads a fork with a chunk of pancake dripping with syrup.

"Maybe," he says as he chews. "Maybe I'll go down to Illinois."

"And follow your Frank Macomber," I say.

"Wouldn't that be something?" he says, but he already seems disinterested in the notion. Or at least disinterested in talking about it.

"These are swell pancakes, Meelie. How's your sandwich?"

"It's tasty, but not as good as the ones you brought to our picnic on the lake."

"Those were special Hemingstein sandwiches. You can't get those in a diner."

I laugh and have another bite as Ernest wipes up some of the syrup from his plate with a slice of bread. Eating is a great pleasure to him. I think that sometimes even breathing must seem like a great pleasure to him. And meeting people and entertaining them—he has that great facility. I'm more solitary and I do well enough with that, but his friendship is an unexpected addition and a welcome one for my time in Chicago. He's like a playful and cherished younger brother. My time with Ernest is a healthy balance to the time I spend with mother and my devotion to studies.

When the waitress comes back to check on us, she smiles at Ernest, whose grin has obviously charmed her. He orders cherry pie and I decide to have a slice, too. When in Hemingstein do as Hemingstein does! While he consumes his pie happily, I glance around the diner and enjoy the sound of feet up and down aisles and the hum of conversations that sound more like birds chirping than clear human words. I listen to the clanging of silverware and watch Ernest happily eating pie, and I think that I might remember this little diner all my life.

After we eat, Ernest seems energized and his smile is perpetual. The food and warm booth have rejuvenated me, too. The hum of conversations all around us is our orchestra. Hem and I are the players in a stage play.

"Let's go see the lake, Meelie. What do you say?"

"Is it a good day to go?" I say, a little skeptically.

"Sure it is. On a day like today, it might be an angry little sea."

"And that's good, Hem? An angry sea?"

"Of course." He grins devilishly. "The waves might be high and crashing. Might be worth the walk."

"I think that would remind you of Michigan."

"It might. I miss Michigan already."

"Then perhaps we must look at the angry sea," I say.

It's a short walk to the lake, and the weather is still holding. Even the sun peeks out from behind massive gray clouds here and there.

"Look at those waves," he says.

"I'm looking. They're grand."

"It's no day for a small boat."

"And yet you would go out anyway, wouldn't you, Hem?"

"I might," he says with conviction.

Clearly the possibility of sailing on an angry sea is tempting to this boy.

"How's your mother, Meelie?"

"She's fine. And your mother? Did she visit your game yesterday?"

"No. She's pregnant."

"Really, Hem?"

"Yes."

He smiles and I'm not sure if it's genuine or manufactured.

"Another sister, Hem?" I say, a bit of tease in my voice.

"That would be my luck alright." He chuckles, perhaps thinking he needs to soften the statement.

"Or maybe you'll have a brother," I say. "Would you like a little brother?"

"Sure I would. But the age difference would be awkward. By the time I'm out of high school, he'd still be a baby."

"But you two would catch up later in life, Hem. You could go watch him play football some day."

"I guess. We'll see."

"When does the baby come, Hem?"

"In the spring. April or May, I guess."

"It's good your father is a doctor," I say.

He nods, looks back out at the lake.

"But he'll be a bundle of nerves," he says. "He was when Carol was born."

"But a doctor overcomes nerves, Hem."

He nods.

"Are we good friends, Meelie?"

"Of course we are."

"Why don't you have friends at school?"

I stare out at the lake for a moment and watch waves crashing on the sand.

"It's a matter of resources, really," I say. "Allocating resources."

He arches his eyebrows.

"I don't know what you mean, Meelie."

"I'm on a schedule, Hem. This is where I am now. But soon enough, I'll be out east, in college. So I allocate my time—to Mother. To my studies."

"And to me."

"Yes, Hem. And to you."

"I'm your Chicago friend."

"You're my Chicago friend. But a real friend."

"That's good, Meelie. For a bit I thought you had no friends at all."

His voice is serious, but I'm not offended.

"For now, Hem, I have what I need."

He nods, seems to assess the validity of my claim.

"I'll miss you when you're gone, Meelie."

"I'll miss you, too, Hem. But no matter where we are, we'll still be friends. Distance does not change that."

"Distance just makes it impossible."

"No," I say. "Don't think that. Distance will make people think all the fonder of people they know and treasure."

He grins, appears to enjoy that sentiment.

"I think that must be true, Meelie. Just like how Michigan is distant, but I know it's still there."

"Exactly, Hem. And when someone is in your heart, they are never far away at all."

We walk back toward Michigan Avenue and Hem is silent at first, lost in thought. I listen to the wind, which has come up in some force. The wind has caught a piece of half-crumpled paper across the street and sends it dancing along, into an alley and out of sight.

"Soon enough it will be Christmas," he says abruptly. "And Thanksgiving is almost here."

"A lovely time, the holidays," I say. "In Atchison, we had gorgeous dinners with lots of people. Very grand. A lovely chandelier above the table, a fire in the fireplace."

"Will you go there, Meelie?"

"I don't know. I must discuss it with mother. I was there, in Atchison, this past summer."

"Did you swim, Meelie?"

"Plenty of times."

"We swim all the time in Michigan. Sometimes our little beach makes me think I am off on a desert island sometimes – marooned, maybe, in the Caribbean."

"It would be no fun to be marooned on an island," I say.

"I know, Meelie. But eventually I am rescued."

"Lucky you. Your dream is truly a dream and not a nightmare."

"Do you have nightmares, Meelie?"

"Not many. Sometimes. Everyone does. How about you?"

"Yes," he says, looking down at his feet as we walked. "I try not to think about them too much."

"That's best. Are they so bad?"

"Sometimes." He glances at me, seriously, then his face breaks into the magnificent grin. "But nightmares go away quickly."

"Don't let them bite you, Hem."

"It's just that I have a lot of imagination."

"I know you do. Maybe more than most people."

"Is that good, Meelie?"

"It's splendid. It will take you far."

"I aim to go far."

Very true, I think. This boy surely is headed somewhere. Am I? I think so. I hope so. I hope very much. But it's frustrating to not know what comes next. This is a stop in my journey. And I have realized I need Ernest's friendship while I'm here. It's as if there's something unseen and undefined and impossible to articulate that is generated and which coats us both as we move forward to our destinies.

"Do you like letters, Hem?"

"I like words. And letters have plenty of them."

"Then I shall write you a letter."

"But we don't live so far apart."

"But a letter is tangible proof of friendship," I say. "Don't you agree?"

The grin holds his face hostage.

"Makes perfect sense," he says.

"Of course it does, Hemingstein. I shall write you this week."

"We could meet next week and you could hand deliver it," he says.

"I can't come next week, Hem. I have plans with mother."

He is disappointed, but tries to hide it, yet his face does not entirely succeed.

"I understand, Meelie."

"It's been some time since I got Mother out and about. I must do it."

"Sure. It will be good for her."

"I just hope the weather holds a bit longer, Hem."

"It might. I'll see what I can do about that."

"Now you control the weather, Hem?"

"My powers are almost unlimited."

"Did you create the angry sea?"

"Yes—and with one hand tied behind my back."

"Yes—because you're the Great Hemingstein."

"I am." He laughs and seems quite satisfied with himself.

He seems to stand taller for a moment, and then we walk some more and reach Michigan Avenue.

"I must go, Hemingstein."

"Me, too."

"Look for my letter."

"I will."

I smile and impulsively touch his cheek.

"You are a sweet boy," I say. "And my dear friend."

"Always, Meelie."

I turn and walk south and I don't glance back at all because I'm sure Ernest is still there, smiling.

## Decay

*I feel it all around me on this island.*

*Creeping decay.*

*Creeping like the inevitable crabs.*

*Creeping perhaps faster than the crab legions.*

*Perhaps more insistent than crab legions.*

*I shake my head.*

*I have been without water for some time now.*

*How long?*

*I don't know.*

*Time has become liquid.*

*Liquid?*

*Time has become water?*

*Is that right?*

*Oh how I wish time was indeed water.*

*Washing over me.*

*Lifting me.*

*I would swim in time.*

*I shake my head again.*

*And start over:*

*Time has become – liquid.*

*I must shake my head again.*

*Vigorously.*

*Time is – liquid.*

*I try to get up.*

*But realize I must sit for now.*

*No choice, really.*

*Gravity wins, rules.*

*I shake my head again.*

*I try again:*

*Time is – fluid.*

*That's better.*

*Or at least different.*

*Different is better.*

*But how much better?*

*How do I measure better?*

*If I can't measure time?*

*What is time, now?*

*To me.*

*The citizen of Amelia Island.*

*What once was Fred Noonan Island.*

*I must own this island.*

*It is surely owning me.*

*I close my eyes:*

*Darkness in the blazing day.*

*Respite.*

*Refuge.*

*Time goes by.*

*How much time?*

*How would I know?*

*I can't measure time.*

*Time is – no, I won't fall into that trap again.*

*Is it a trap?*

*Or mirage?*

*Disaster?*

*Don't be silly.*

*Time is merely time.*

*It's neither fluid or liquid.*

*Or disaster.*

*It's just time.*

*In my dream I am home.*

*Back in Atchison.*

*I'm a child.*

*The air is fresh, sweet.*

*It comes like that off the Missouri River.*

*The muddy river is far below the bluff, crowned by the house.*

*The house squats handsomely overlooking the river.*

*Surrounded by a fence.*

*Shaded by tall trees.*

*Two stone dogs guard the paved walk and porch entrance.*

*Tall wooden pillars support the porch.*

*I can hear the crackle in the fireplace.*

*I can see the gleaming china and silver on the dining room table.*

*Light showers down from the crystal chandelier above us.*

*Grace is said.*

*And Grandmother Otis sets about serving fluffy mashed potatoes.*

*And steaming thick brown gravy.*

*Heaven.*

# Letter

*Despite the recent skirmish, I allow myself to slip away yet again into the past:*

It was a Tuesday, I think, when I sat down to write my letter to Ernest. I didn't write the letter in our apartment, but instead at the little diner near our apartment that Ernest and I once ate in. I thought it would be an ideal location, since we both had been there. And we were such diner people! It was not as crowded or noisy as the diner on Michigan Avenue. I sipped coffee and thought for a time about the blustery early November weather and then I wrote:

Dear Hemingstein,

I must thank you again for another lovely journey to the lake. It's such a grand lake and your company is grand, too. You really are my true Chicago friend. I think of you like a brother, an ideal younger brother. Even though I look forward very much to going to college soon, I know a part of me will come to miss hearing about your exploits as you finish school, too. I'm on the verge of entering that big wider world. It's hard to believe it's really just a matter of months before my time here is done - just the winter and spring to get through. You have time yet before that happens and you should savor your school time. Don't be like me — a loner girl! I know you won't. You have the gift of charming people and winning them to your side. I am more solitary. But there is purpose to my solitude, I can assure you. This coming weekend I must spend much time with mother, as I mentioned, but the following Sunday I am free again.

Would you like to meet at the art institute? I have not been there yet and would very much like to see it. Shall we meet first outside the institute, at perhaps 10 o'clock, and have brunch? I am told admission on Sundays is free. I will look for you there, Hem, and will understand if something prevents you from attending.

Meelie

That Sunday it is cold, but still no snow, and I am very pleased to see Ernest waiting outside when I arrive at the art institute.

"Meelie," he calls as he waves enthusiastically.

"Hemingstein—you made it after all."

"Did you think I wouldn't?"

"I don't know. I worried that my letter might have somehow ended up in Africa, or the Orient."

"I got it just fine. But am I your little brother now?"

I pat his elbow lightly.

"Cherished younger brother—how's that?"

"But I'm taller, and filling out fast, Meelie."

"But still younger, Hem. And now definitely like family. Is that somehow bad?"

"Not at all," he says, smiling. "I'd be proud to tell anyone I'm your brother now."

"Brother Hemingstein," I say. "It rather makes you sound like a German monk.

"The Hemingways are English," he says, laughing, and offers his arm and we enter the institute. Inside it's warm and there's a comforting and faintly musty odor. Not unpleasant at all. There is a sense of very old things everywhere and with the ability to reveal much about the past, the world, history, people, the arts, fantasies, realities. We pace ourselves—much to see!

There was much sculpture that I enjoyed—Roman, Greek, Egyptian, Assyrian, Babylonian. There was a collection of Naples Bronzes and much Oriental art and many Egyptian antiquities—a delight!

The second floor exhibits much Medieval and Renaissance art. There is a room with wood carvings that Ernest says made him think of his beloved Michigan. Another room offersd a collection of porcelain I rather admired and enjoyed. There is a painting of the New Mexico landscape that Ernest eyes with much interest. The land in the painting is brown and bare and the horizons stretch forever.

"Pretty different than around here," he says.

As we drifted happily from room to room, our eyes constantly discovering new treasures, certain painting captivated Ernest—El Greco's "Assumption of the Virgin." Perhaps the notion of a virgin held special interest for him. And he lingered at a lovely painting of a heron called "Home of the Heron." There were many herons in Michigan, he explained, and the painting could have been a scene from any of dozens of places that he knew there.

But despite all the many splendid wonders we saw, Ernest proclaimed the bronze lions standing watch on pedestals at the institute's entrance as the best of the whole experience. He was quite taken by the lions, calling them—"Stupendous!"

We lingered at the lions for a time on the way out. His eyes sparkled as he examined every aspect of them. He was quite pleased and deemed them "Magnificent guardians."

Outside the cold was a bit of a shock, but we adjusted to it quickly and walking helped keep us warm.

"Where shall we eat, Hemingstein? Walking in this weather makes me hungry. And I know it must make you positively famished."

"I could eat," he says.

"Astonishing," I say, smiling, too, and his grin manages somehow to become even wider.

"This is your neighborhood," he says. "Show me the way."

"Now I'm the guide?"

"You are. I'm in your hands."

"Then, the little diner we ate in before, Hem. It's not far."

"That's an attractive quality," he says, clapping his hands together a couple times to warm them.

At the diner Ernest holds the door open for me and soon we are quite cozy and warm in a booth with hot coffee.

Ernest raises his coffee cup for a toast:

"To lions," he says. "To the wonderful lions."

"To the magnificent lions," I say, and we click our cups together, spilling coffee and laughing as we sop it up with napkins.

"They'll throw us out, if we aren't careful," I say.

"If they do, they'll have to answer to the lions," he says playfully. "I'll loose the lions on them."

"Yes—you must."

We order our late lunch and Ernest is in rare form, asking for roast beef and au gratin potatoes and gravy to be poured over the beef and a side of mashed potatoes, too. I order the same, minus the mashed potatoes. I am saving room for pie because I know Ernest will want some.

"A stupendous feast," he proclaims after finishing his slice of apple pie. I am still working at mine, but enjoying it. He leans back in the booth, quite satisfied.

"Cold today, isn't it, Meelie?"

"Quite," I say with my last bite of pie. "But no snow yet."

"Any time now," he says. "Any old time."

"But maybe not today, Hem. I'd prefer not today."

"Why? Snow is inevitable."

"Yes—but if it waits until at least tomorrow, I'll have more time to be ready for it."

"How much more ready could you become?" he asks.

"Oh, oodles. A day makes a difference in just about anything."

"If you say so, Meelie."

"I do say so, Hemingstein."

He arches his eyebrows comically.

"Then it's settled," he says. "No snow today."

"Quite settled," I say as I sip my coffee.

"Wasn't the institute stupendous?" he says.

"It was, Hem. Is stupendous your word for today?"

"I think so. As a word, stupendous is – stupendous!"

"Like the lions?"

"Exactly—stupendous!"

"You love those lions, Hem."

"I do. Some day I'll see real lions—in Africa."

"I don't doubt it."

"The world is amazing, Meelie. I want to see it."

"Me, too."

"All of it."

"You shall, Hem."

"You get to go first," he says. "I'm stuck here a few more years yet."

"Is it so bad?"

"Naw. I have fun. I have Michigan in the summers. It's a swell place."

"Walloon Lake, is it?"

"Yes."

"It sounds so lovely," I say.

"It's the last good country."

"Endure winter and embrace summer," I say.

He smiles. Already he is likely planning next summer in Michigan. Next summer I will have left Chicago. It's a tantalizing thought, but tempered by the fact I know I will miss Ernest. My unexpected friend.

"So, Hem, did you really like my letter?"

"Truly. I did."

"I shall send you another."

"Stupendous!"

"My letters aren't *that* good, Hem."

"But they are. The one, anyway."

"How good?"

"Stupendous!"

I can't help but laugh. How will the world ever contain this boy?

"Well, I will write another, even if it won't be stupendous."

"Do you like to write letters, Meelie?"

"I do. It's a way to be exact."

He nods.

"I know what you mean," he says. "There's something about writing. I've been reading a lot in school. It makes me think of writing something."

"What have you been reading, Hem?"

"Poetry. Stuff in the Bible. I read Jane Austen. I read *Pride and Prejudice*."

"Really. How did you like it?"

"It was a swell love story—stupendous!"

We both laugh.

"But Mr. Darcy is a bit of a dude," he says, chuckling.

"How did you like Elizabeth Bennett?"

"She was swell."

"Stupendous, Hem?"

"Truly stupendous! But her mother—that's another story."

"What's wrong with Mrs. Bennett?"

He shrugs his shoulders.

"She reminds me of my mother," he says quietly.

"But Mrs. Bennett is comical, Hem. Is your mother?"

"No," he says, looking away at the counter. "I wouldn't call her that."

"And now she's having a baby," I say.

"Yes," he says, looking away again. "Another little Christian soldier."

"Maybe it will be a brother."

His face brightens.

"Maybe. By the time we head north, we'll know, I guess."

"Cheer up, Hem. Boy, or girl, it will look up to you as a stupendous older brother."

He grins.

"Stupendous!"
Such a boy!

## Existence

*I searched the island a long time.*
*Nearly gave up.*
*Nearly passed out.*
*Nearly.*
*But did not.*
*And then I found it:*
*Water.*
*More valuable than gold.*
*In the crook of a tree.*
*Enough to revive me.*
*Enough to save me.*
*For now.*
*What is now?*
*How long is now?*
*How shall I define now?*
*Does now lead to the future?*
*Does now lead anywhere?*
*And how shall I define future?*
*Or past?*

*The past is known.*

*It happened.*

*Existed.*

*Can be recalled.*

*And can't be taken away.*

*For long, anyway.*

*The past is real.*

*Even though it's over.*

*What an odd thought.*

*But the past I can count on.*

*It's my only refuge.*

*Lovely refuge.*

*The future is unknown.*

*Is it?*

*Can I not figure out the last act?*

*Of this play with only one character?*

*Stop.*

*Stop thinking that way.*

*Just stop.*

*Right now.*

*You found water.*

*You will find it again.*

*And next you will find food.*

*Even if only a bite or two.*

*A crab scout will stray too close and you will have it.*

*That will make future real again.*

*At least for a time.*

*And that's what I do:*

*I sustain myself longer.*

*And longer.*

*I survive.*

*Somehow.*

*I live tenuously.*

*I wait.*

*Expectantly.*

*I hope.*

*Excessively.*

*I sleep.*

*Fitfully.*

*I dream.*

*Endlessly.*

*I live.*

*For now.*

# A Thanksgiving As Interesting As Could Be

*Off I go:*

The week after our visit to the art institute I sat down in the little diner after school and wrote Ernest another letter:

Dear Stupendous Hemingstein!

Wasn't the art institute grand? So many treasures! I enjoyed it immensely. Your lions were marvelous. Or should I say—stupendous! I can just imagine you even dreaming about the lions. I bet you did. Tell me the truth when next I see you. Or maybe you already described the stupendous lions to all your friends—perhaps as even taller than they really are? I described them to mother. I kept them to their regular sizes, but added that they are indeed marvelous. And I told her about all the paintings and sculptures—the magnificent heron we saw that reminded you of lovely Michigan and Walloon Lake.

Mother and I have plans for the coming weekend. And I have a school project to focus on. You know me—ever so working hard to be done and looking ahead to college. But my time here in Chicago has become all the more fun and unexpected at that because we are friends. Our adventures have been, well—stupendous!

Why not write me a letter back, Hemingstein? You mentioned that you have been reading a lot and even thinking some about writing—here's your chance! Allow me to challenge you! A friendly challenge, of course. Motivation from a friend. Let me know how your week goes and maybe soon we can explore the city again, or even the lake, weather permitting.

Meelie

After I had mailed the letter I walked home. It was cold, but not unbearably so. I had certainly gotten used to it and my wool coat served me well. And thank goodness there was no breeze to make it colder. But as I turned down the street we lived on, it began to snow. I stopped a moment to watch: delicate, small flakes descended, and there was stillness in the air that was not sad at all but rather serene.

Hem's reply came some days later:

Meelie:
The Great Hemingstein sends you greetings!—stop.
Isn't the snow grand?--stop.
It's stupendous!—stop.
How do you like my telegram style?—stop.
Thanksgiving at Hemingstein Castle approaches!—stop.
Please come to dinner with us and bring your mother—stop.
My parents say you are welcome—stop.
My sisters would love to meet you—stop.
Don't stop—please say you will come.
The Great Hemingstein!
Now I must stop!
But you must not stop!
Come to our castle!

Mother declined to attend the Hemingway Thanksgiving. I was not much surprised by her stand. She claimed to just be too tired from all the errands and sightseeing we had done recently and just desiring to rest on the holiday, but I knew she just didn't feel up to a house full of strangers and the etiquette and diplomacy and manners that would be required. Too taxing for her. I nearly decided to decline as well, knowing I would be on display and under scrutiny by the Hemingways, but I hated to disappoint Hem. He seemed quite excited about it and I was indeed curious to see for myself what sort of family and home life lay behind such an interesting and energetic boy.

Ernest arranged for his father to pick me up in his black Ford Model T. I confess to finding Dr. Hemingway outwardly pleasant but rather intimidating. He was a tall, dour man on the outside, with an impassive face at first, sad eyes, and a dark beard. At times he looked faintly perplexed about something, but he smiled enthusiastically when we were introduced and he asked about my mother solicitously. I could sense that as a younger man Dr. Hemingway must have been handsome and even now would be again without the beard—and the perplexed looks.

In his dark suit, Dr. Hemingway seemed much more like clergy than physician. And I knew from what Hem had said that the doctor was a conservative man and religious. I could imagine him with a Bible in hand lecturing about virtue. Oak Park, Hem had explained, was a conservative enclave. I don't think Hem saw that as a good thing. At first Dr. Hemingway didn't say much, but perhaps that was because Hem did much of the talking, and it was hard for him to get a word in. His father did ask me about Atchison when I mentioned my own family, and he mentioned having a brother in Kansas City. He even rather spontaneously related to me how his Model T had been stolen earlier in the year, but recovered just the very next day on Chicago's South Side. Odd, I replied to him, but fortunate and he nodded politely. But after the introductions and small talk Dr. Hemingway focused on steering while Hem and I chatted like magpies about our recent walks around Chicago. Along the way Ernest confessed that our visit to the art institute was not his first — as a boy his mother took him and his sisters there, but he pretended it was his first time so as not to detract from the experience.

The Hemingway house was a light gray stucco with lots of windows at the corner of Kenilworth Avenue and Iowa Street, an impressive three-story with servant quarters and an oak tree in the front yard guarding the covered porch. A home that clearly reflected a family of means and substance and station in the community. Compared to other homes around it, the Hemingway house seems to be—more energetic.

As we got out and walked to the door I recalled that it was Hem's mother who had designed the house, and I thought that a bit unusual; perhaps not odd, but a little unconventional for the time, yet I liked hearing about a woman operating in what was decidedly a man's territory. I would soon learn from Hem that Dr. Hemingway did the shopping and even much of the cooking in the Hemingway household—he even oversaw the servants—while Mrs. Hemingway spent much time painting and on her music, the house having a music studio and recital hall just for her. And her name—she hyphenated her name! It was Grace Hall-Hemingway. Quite something for those days. I was nervous to meet her, but curious nonetheless.

I met the sisters first—Marcelline, Ursula, Madeline, and little Carol. They converged quickly, magically, from different parts of the cavernous home. They were a happy lot, eager to meet me, I suppose, because I was nearly grown up and maybe they wondered what an older sister would be like instead of an older brother. And because I was Ernest's mysterious friend, too, I surmised. They had good manners and asked me about mother, and I explained that she had recently been ill—something of a falsehood, though also technically true. I said that she really just needed rest and that she sent her most grateful thanks for the invitation and that was certainly true. And really, it was not a conversation desperate for details or substance. Then the girls ran off to fetch coats and go outside for a spell as there was plenty of time before dinner.

Mrs. Hemingway abruptly appeared in a hallway, rather like an apparition, I confess. She was a robust woman featuring a large head and plump face and whitening hair in a bun atop her head. She wore a dark flowing Victorian dress that made her seem a bit theatrical, like an actress in a play. I recalled Hem saying she was now pregnant, but I could not really tell anything due to the dress and her overall size. I felt I should dare not ask about it, of course. She was smiling broadly and hugged me as we were introduced, then she, too, asked about Mother. Then she steered me to her studio, which was spacious, had a vaulted ceiling and even a little balcony. This was where she gave lessons and composed her own music, I was told, which was actually sold through a company and made money. I learned that in addition to Madison Square Garden in New York, she had performed in Los Angeles. Quite amazing! Mrs. Hemingway was not like any woman I had known.

The studio was a thirty-by-thirty foot affair and its centerpiece was a Steinway grand piano. She smiled very grandly and proudly as my eyes surveyed the room. On a wall was a life-sized portrait of a man – her great great grandfather, she explained.

"William Miller Hall," she says. "It is believed that he studied with the great Paganini."

"I'm afraid my music education is limited, Mrs. Hemingway."

"Well, he was Italian, of course. Perhaps the greatest of the violinists."

"Oh," I say. "How very interesting."

"Ernest practices his cello here," Mrs. Hemingway says.

"I didn't know he played," I say. "He didn't mention it."

"No, I don't guess he would have." She wrinkled her nose slightly, as if annoyed. "His father plays cornet."

"Do they play well?"

"They practice regularly."

"Practice makes perfect," I say.

She nods, smiles thinly. "We are a musical family."

"And capable of a home symphony," I say, a little anxious to utter the appropriate reply. "How wonderful. And what do you all play?"

"Hymns, of course—and I'm partial to Gilbert and Sullivan."

"How much fun that must be," I say.

"Yes, indeed, Amelia. But Ernest and his father tend to play a little off-key."

"Oh, no. But I'm sure you guide them, Mrs. Hemingway."

"You may call me Grace, child. And, yes—I do instruct them."

"You may call me Meelie, if you like—Ernest does."

"Oh does he?"

"I think I'm like an older sister to him," I say.

"Really? And does he have you already in his little world of nicknames as well?" Grace asks.

I nod.

"He likes to be called Hem," I say.

"Yes, indeed he does. I have noticed."

I try to change the subject.

"You have given your family much culture, Grace."

She seems pleased by the compliment.

"I believe I started them off right," she says. "I have exposed them to opera, symphonies, the museums, the theater. These are essential aspects of an education."

"Indeed," I say, not exactly sure what to say. "And Ernest tells me he has become a reader."

"Yes," she says. "He has read *Ivanhoe* and *Robinson Crusoe*, and some of the better boy's magazines, such as *Might and Main*. I encourage his reading, of course."

"And Jane Austen," I say. "He recently told me he had read *Pride and Prejudice*."

"He's read Austen has he?" she says. She seems to ponder it a moment.

"Yes. But he said Mr. Darcy seemed a bit of a dude."

"He would think that," she says, frowning ever so slightly. "Ernest must learn to focus more."

"He's young," I say, immediately regretting what might easily seem to be overstepping her role as mother.

"He's approaching sixteen," she says, a hint of frustration in her voice.

I nod and smile sweetly, but say nothing. There's a long pause, and I glance about the room while she seems to compose herself. After the tour of her music room, she gives me a tour of much of the rest of the grand house, and then we convene in a parlor with Mr. Hemingway and Ernest. Mr. Hemingway does not offer to be addressed as Clarence, but he is ever so pleasant.

"Did you enjoy the tour, Miss Earhart?" he says as though we had just that moment met.

"Indeed I did. The house is grand."

"Excellent," he says. "We are happy to have you as our guest."

"You can call me Amelia, Mr. Hemingway. Or even Meelie."

"Meelie?"

"Her nickname," Ernest says abruptly.

"I picked that up as a child," I say. "It seems to have stuck."

"Amelia," Mr. Hemingway says. "It's a fine name."

He nods and smiles and there is an awkward moment as Ernest looks at me and Grace smoothes her dress absently.

"It's a grand name," Ernest says, looking again at me and smiling broadly to offer support.

"And so you met Ernest just walking about downtown, Meelie?" Grace says with a pinch of skepticism in her voice.

"At a diner," I say. "On Michigan Avenue."

"It's a swell diner," Ernest says. "It's very clean and down by the Tribune Building."

"A diner," Grace says as though weighing the concept of such a place.

"That's very—public," Mr. Hemingway says with a neutral voice.

"But a very pleasant diner," I say.

"I'm sure it is." Mr. Hemingway nods, seems satisfied with my answer. "And the diner food?"

"Filling," I say. "Hearty."

"Very good," Mr. Hemingway says. Food, I recall, is one of his family responsibilities.

"I should like to think we serve ample and filling food here at home," Grace says, her voice rising ever so slightly.

Mr. Hemingway looks at her with one of his perplexed looks.

Ernest seems suddenly uncharacteristically subdued in the presence of his parents. Silence settles in for a long moment, and then the sisters abruptly parade back into the house and through the parlor slipping off coats and proclaiming it a chilly day.

"Oh, it's not that cold," Ernest says and abruptly he rises from his chair. "Why don't we have a look outside, Meelie?"

"If you like," I say, relieved to escape the tension of the parlor.

Mr. and Mrs. Hemingway smile, but say nothing, and Ernest and I retrieve our coats and go outdoors, where it is indeed chilly, but a relief from being under the scrutiny of strangers. We walk along Kenilworth Avenue for a couple of blocks. The cold is preferable to sitting with Hem's parents in the parlor.

"It *is* cold today," Ernest says. "But not so bad."

"We're used to walking in it, Hem."

"And maybe it's not as cold out here as back in the parlor."

"It was not so bad," I say. "I'm a stranger to them."

"It seemed like a cool reception to me," he says.

"Your parents were just being parents – and they're mindful I am a little older than you."

"I guess so, Meelie. I confess they're an odd pair sometimes."

After a bit I say, "Your mother's music room is so grand."

"She rules the roost alright."

I sense a bit of a growing chasm between Ernest and Grace, but also that they have much in common in their personalities. Perhaps there is much competition between them for the air in a room.

"She first introduced you to your stupendous lions, Hem."

He smiles and his face brightens.

"Stupendous!"

"That's the spirit, Hemingstein."

"Now let's go back before we freeze," he says.

Dinner is quite the nice affair around a large table. I offer to help with dinner in some way, but Mr. Hemingway insists I sit and enjoy myself. He even pulls out my chair for me and good-naturedly reminds Hem that he's the one who should be doing it. Once the table is set, there's a prayer by Mr. Hemingway and the moment is quite solemn. But afterwards the girls, especially, are very lively, and Ernest helps move the food around the table. There is a very plump turkey, perhaps the biggest I have ever seen, and Mr. Hemingway has meticulously handled cooking the dinner, which features a huge tureen of mashed potatoes and there is also thick gravy and dressing and yams and oyster casserole. Pies and even a chocolate cake are our dessert. It's sumptuous and I wish mother might have attended, but I suspect she would not have mixed well or comfortably with this family.

Mr. Hemingway assures me that he will put aside a generous sampling of it all for me to take home and share with Mother, and in this kind gesture I begin to get past the stern exterior and glimpse his kindness. It wants out but has trouble peeking out sometimes. Perhaps he has trouble blossoming while his wife absorbs and demands so much time.

"How does all this compare to the little diner downtown, Meelie?" Grace asks.

"No comparison," I say between spoonfuls of mashed potatoes. "It's quite wonderful," I add nodding toward Mr. Hemingway, who smiles sweetly and, I think, quite genuinely for the first time that I have seen.

Across from me Ernest beams as he happily devours potatoes and turkey with gravy.

"Mr. Hemingway is quite a good cook," Grace says without looking at her husband, and it sounds rather odd to me all of a sudden, but I smile and nod enthusiastically. With a quick glance I see Mr. Hemingway's perplexed look. It dissolves quickly when he offers turkey to take home.

"It's kind of you, Mr. Hemingway, to send some of this home with me—Mother will appreciate it."

"Think nothing of it," he says, smiling. "We have plenty."

I see that Mr. Hemingway is perhaps much more a man of action than words. Grace seems much more about words—and drama.

And Ernest, I think, clearly favors his father, shares his father's love of action, and yet ironically his temperament leans more toward that of his mother. He chafes under her rule, I begin to see, and yet he is more like her than perhaps he even would admit. How interesting. I fear that some sort of confrontation is coming between them as he gets older and as she grows impatient with him. I wonder what she expects of him for the future. Music, perhaps? Well, if he plays off-key, perhaps that is not to be. And I simply do not see

Ernest as a musician. He is bright, talented—but more inclined to outdoors than indoors, I think.

I let those thoughts go, accept a generous slice of chocolate cake, which Mr. Hemingway seems to much enjoy serving it and seeing me eat. It really is quite good cake. It melts nicely in my mouth and the chocolate helps wash away my nervousness. I know that Mother will enjoy the cake most of all. I believe I am beginning to take the measure of Mr. Hemingway and I like him, despite his outward formality.

After the wonderful dinner, Ernest talks me into another walk, which I welcome for the exercise and the chance to catch my breath from trying so hard to mind my manners and be friendly. Grace disappears, but Mr. Hemingway expresses concern that I will be warm enough as I slip into my coat.

It does not seem so cold at all at first because we have been inside so long where the great food has warmed us, too. We walk again down Kenilworth, in the other direction, this time.

"Did you get enough to eat," Ernest asks.

"I'm stuffed, Hem. Like the turkey."

He laughs.

"It was a swell dinner."

"Stupendous?" I say.

"Yes—stupendous."

"It was good of you to ask me, Hem. Thank you."

"We're pals, Meelie. Pals take care of each other."

"They do. But it was most generous of you."

"What did you think of the Hemingway clan?" he says.

"Wonderful hosts. Your sisters are quite the group."

"Yeah," he says, looking down as we walk. "But how'd it go in the music studio?"

"A grand room. I enjoyed it."

"Not what I meant, Meelie. How'd it go with my mother?"

"She explained Paganini to me."

"Not that again," he says.

"What's wrong with Paganini?"

"Never met the man," he says a bit harshly.

"But your ancestor studied with him. A great honor, I take it."

"If true."

"It's not true?"

He shrugs his shoulders and grimaces a little.

"Maybe it is, maybe it isn't."

"Your mother seems to think it is."

"Well, then, it must be so," he says sarcastically. "Anyway, one fiddler is the same as another to me."

"Music won't be your career, Hem?"

He stops and stares at me rather thunderstruck.

"Did she say that?"

"No." I hesitate. "She said you play off-key."

He smirks.

"Now *there's* something that *is* true."

We turn and head back.

"She seems happy that you read a lot, Hem."

"How did it come up?"

"I mentioned you'd read Austen."

He smirks again.

"How'd she take to that?"

"She actually seemed a little surprised."

"I wonder if *she's* read *Pride and Prejudice*," he says.

"How about your father," I say. "Do you think he's read it?"

"Not at all," he says.

"Grace says you liked *Ivanhoe* and *Robinson Crusoe*."

"Oh, it's Grace now, is it?"

"She asked me to call her that."

"I see. Now you two are thick as thieves, I guess."

"Not at all, Hemingstein. But I must be polite."

He nods faintly.

"I suppose so."

"And *did* you like *Ivanhoe* and *Robinson Crusoe*, Hem?"

"They're okay. I liked Mark Twain better."

"Yes, I think you would."

"What does that mean?"

"Twain would maybe be closer to your heart. Huck Finn and Tom Sawyer and all that."

"It's a swell book alright," he says.

We are back at the house. Both of us hesitate to go inside. There's not so much light left in the day, and I know it's time to go home. Mother will be happy to see me, and I will enjoy treating her with lovely cake.

"What will you do for Christmas, Meelie?"

"We may go to Atchison. I don't know. I must ask Mother again. But maybe we will. How will Christmas be at Hemingstein Castle?"

He grins.

"More people. Louder. A big dinner, of course."

"Sounds lovely."

"What will Atchison be like?" he says.

"Very much the same. Lots of people and much good food. I look forward to that, if that's what we end up doing."

"Do you think that's what you'll do, Meelie?"

"Very possibly. We must also check on father, in Kansas City."

We slip inside and take off our coats, but Mr. Hemingway very politely reminds us of the waning daylight. Soon are off in the Model T after I say goodbye to Grace and the sisters and on the drive to Hyde Park Mr. Hemingway seems to be more free to be himself and chat, and the three of us have a pleasant drive as a few stray snowflakes flutter to the ground.

Ernest walks me to the door of my building.

"It was swell of you to come, Meelie."

"And swell of you to ask me."

I impulsively hug him, and after he looks away. I think that despite the bluster and energy and his many activities, he is a lonely boy.

"I may not see you for a while, Hem."

"I know."

"But I'll write you a letter," I say.

"You must."

"And I will."

He smiles bravely, though his eyes are moist. I squeeze his arm and then turn and go. I hear the door to the motorcar shut and it chugs away.

# Chocolate Cake

*I am back from the past.*

*The lovely past.*

*The safe past.*

*The past full of life.*

*It's a glorious journey.*

*Visiting the past.*

*A refuge.*

*Dear refuge!*

*But taxing, too.*

*And always.*

*I am back.*

*On this island.*

*Spent from the trek into the past.*

*And always.*

*The crabs.*

*Always the crabs.*

*Always, always, always.*

*The crabs.*

*Crabs everywhere!*

*Their spies keep track of me.*

*Shadow me.*

*Track me.*

*I kill a spy and eat it!*

*Moisture.*

*Food.*

*Life.*

*I can live some more.*

*But I think of cake.*

*Chocolate cake.*

*Moist chocolate cake.*

*Rich chocolate cake.*

*Cake at the Hemingways.*

*Hemingway cake.*

*Mr. Hemingway's cake.*

*It's all I can think of for a while.*

*Then I recall that Thanksgiving.*

*The Hemingway Thanksgiving.*

*The dinner.*

*The lovely dinner.*

*Turkey.*

*Mashed potatoes.*

*Stupendous!*

*If only I could hear Ernest say that.*

*One more time.*

*Stupendous!*

*I look around.*

*This island is not stupendous.*

*But Ernest was.*

*Though I never saw him again.*

*After I left Chicago.*

*In 1915.*

*Ages ago.*

*Centuries ago.*

*Another life ago.*

*Many lives ago.*

*Many people ago.*

*Many flights ago.*

*I rise, slowly.*

*Gingerly.*

*Off I go.*

*With much effort.*

*I do find a little water.*

*And it lifts me.*

*Lift is flight.*

*I can go on some more.*

*But I want cake.*

*Chocolate cake.*

# The Year of Departure

*The past awaits, and eagerly I fall back into it:*

I did not see Ernest again until after Christmas and months into the New Year—1915. A year of coming departure from Chicago. A year of departure from school into a wider world. Much snow had fallen and gone and been replaced by new snow. I wrote Ernest several times before and after Christmas and he wrote back in his usual enthusiastic style. Stupendous! By March the winter was weakening and we arranged to meet at our little diner on Michigan Avenue.

Far down the street I can see him already out front, doing that funny thing he does of rolling back and forth on the balls of his large feet. He doesn't see me right away as he surveys the street scene in the other direction. He is like a boulder in the flow of human traffic on Michigan Avenue. Or, perhaps more like one of those gorgeous bronze lions standing guard at the entrance to the art institute. Those lions are *his* lions, and I think, in a funny but true way, he is one of them.

He turns and sees me: the magnificent grin appears in a flash. He waves and lumbers toward me. I think he has grown another inch, or maybe it's just been too long since I saw him. He won't remain a boy much longer. He leans heavily toward manhood. When he reaches me there is an awkward moment, but then we both extend arms and realize we must hug.

"How are you, Meelie?"

"Stupendous!"

He laughs and rocks again on the balls of his feet.

"And you, Hemingstein? Did you survive the winter?"

"I took to it like a duck to water."

"Colorful. And how are your parents?"

"Fine, Meelie."

"And Mr. Hemingway—he is well?"

"Both are doing okay."

"Oh—and your mother," I say. "How soon does the baby come?"

"Quite soon," he says.

"Goodness! She must be quite large by now."

"She's huge. We're all curious to know what we'll have."

"The sisters must want another sister," I say. "Only natural."

"I think they'd like another brother. But I can't swear to it."

"Maybe they try and deceive you, Hem."

"I wouldn't put it past them."

"And you, Hem—would you like a brother?"

"Sure I would." But he sounds faintly undecided, as though not quite sure how he should feel if it is a brother. I think he has gotten used to sisters.

"Don't fret about the age difference," I say. "It all evens out eventually."

"I guess so." He suddenly looks somewhat overwhelmed by the coming addition to the family, but the look quickly washes from his face and the magnificent grin reappears.

"I'm hungry, Meelie. Let's go in."

"You're always hungry, Hemingstein."

"I'm a growing boy."

"You seem taller, Hem. Are you?"

"I am. And filling out some more." He pats his stomach. "I'll make my move at football in the fall. You watch."

"I wish I could." I regret saying anything at all that signals I won't be around in the fall. He smiles back bravely.

We find an empty booth and hang our coats on the rack. Warm coffee arrives. I look at Ernest and smile. It's so good to see him after so long. It really was a long winter in some ways. I stayed home mostly and spent time with mother when not finishing schoolwork. The term will be over soon and high school will end. I can hardly wait. Eager to go into the world and find myself, yet I am very happy to see Ernest, and I know how much I will miss him. He is journeying toward something, as I am, and he will be fine. Both of us will get to where we are supposed to be. It's the natural order of things. The pattern of reality.

We order breakfast, as it's still early enough. Hem has flapjacks and eggs and toast with butter and jam. I order a ham omelet and toast, too. I am adopting Hem's view that walking begets eating well, and in eating well one lives life well. I predict that once beyond sleepy Oak Park, Ernest will dedicate himself to living well. He seems a natural for it.

"Almost forgot," he says as he chews his toast. "My father says to tell you hello."

"How kind of him, Hem. I like your father."

He nods and chews some more.

"I like my father, too."

"Of course you do."

"What did you think of my mother, Meelie? Looking back, I mean."

I sip coffee to buy time and think a moment.

"A talented woman."

"I don't mean about music," he says.

"Well, I certainly admire women who make their mark, Hem."

"But did you like her?"

"She was very courteous to me."

"That's not the same thing."

"But I met her just once," I say. "And it was a hectic day for her."

"I suppose."

"How are you getting along with her, Hem?"

"She likes to ride me." He shrugs. "She likes her rules."

I decide to change the subject.

"Summer's not so far off, Hem. Your beloved Walloon Lake awaits."

That draws a smile out of him.

"You should see it, Meelie."

"I know it must be ever so grand, Hem. If you say it's grand, I know it must be."

"This weather will break in our favor soon," he says. "Then it really will be close to summer."

"And the Hemingways will journey north, to lovely Michigan," I say. "And with a new family member."

"It will be odd," he says, looking slightly confused for just a few seconds. "A baby at the cottage. It's been a while since we had that."

"A baby livens a house, I was always told."

He grins.

"Is that some sort of Atchison saying?"

"It's true everywhere, Hem."

"And how *was* Atchison, Meelie, and your Christmas?"

"Divine. I saw much family. And we ate well— you would have liked that part."

"That's the best part of Christmas."

"That and family," I say.

"How has school been?" he says.

"It's nearly done. Thank goodness. Just a short time to go."

"You want to be free," he says.

"I do. And see more of the world."

"I'll second that," he says, finishing the last of the flapjacks.

"But first you must see Michigan again, Hem. What will you do first at Lake Walloon?"

His face brightens at the prospect.

"Go fishing, of course."

"With your father?"

"At first. Then I'll branch out on my own. To find the out of the way places."

"And see herons, like the one at the art institute, I imagine."

"Of course. And ducks and geese everywhere."

"But the heron stands apart from ducks and geese, I think."

"Like us, Meelie."

"*Do* we stand apart?"

He smiles but still manages to look serious, too.

"We do—stand apart."

"In what way, Hem?"

"We sense things." He runs a hand absently through his hair. "We feel things. We know something's coming." He glances around as though concerned someone might hear a secret. "You know what I mean."

"What's coming, Hem?"

He mulls it a moment.

"Our whole lives."

"But we don't actually know how they will be," I say.

He leans closer across the table and lowers his voice.

"But we can feel that what's coming will be special."

"You mean—stupendous!"

"Yes—stupendous!" he says laughing.

"Is this our secret, Hemingstein?"

He grins and eases back in the booth.

"Maybe it's a prophecy, Meelie."

I laugh. "Now you're being mystical."

"Naw. I'm just thinking out loud."

The waitress stops by our table and Hem charms her with his grin. Already the mysticism is gone, and he's the playful boy again with his whole life before him, and a part of him, though, seems sure it will be momentous. I can't help but think it will. What will he be? And what will I? I feel sure I will turn out okay and find my place, wherever it leads me. All will be revealed.

Hem helps me into my coat and we go outside and walk along Michigan Avenue. We pass through clumps of people, some old, some young—people nearing the end of their destinies, and some just starting toward them. Souls arriving and departing.

"Is winter truly over, Hem?"

"Maybe. I think so. Soon, anyway."

"Then soon we must go to the lake again and have another picnic."

"Stupendous!" he says and we both laugh loudly.

We walk along for a few minutes quietly, just watching people and gazing at buildings, pausing to look down at the sluggish Chicago River. Several motorcars chug by noisily behind us. I touch his arm.

"I shall write you a letter," I say. "This week."

"Maybe the weather will break next week," he says.

"So soon?"

"You never know. Maybe your letter will cause it to break."

"That's silly. Fate doesn't work that way—does it?"

"Maybe. Fate can be influenced, I think."

"In what ways?"

"I'm just being hopeful, Meelie."

"Well, if it's not snowing, and not too cold, maybe we can go to the lake the week after. What does fate say to that?"

"Not next week?" he says.

"I promised Mother."

"A promise is a promise."

Impulsively I kiss Ernest's cheek and he blushes. I felt his tender whiskers.

"Have to go," I say. "But I will write—very soon."

"Don't forget," he says.

"Never."

I turn south and start along Michigan Avenue. We have become quite good and efficient at quick goodbyes. I glance back once, as is my custom, but Ernest has already disappeared into the crowd.

## Thawing

*The portal to the past slips open:*

When I next met Ernest the weather had eased and spring seemed a distinct possibility. Even inevitable. Definitely welcome. We met at our little diner downtown and walked to Lake Michigan. School was winding down for us both. But for me it was coming to an end and for Ernest it was just a year passing, and his thoughts, no doubt, were sometimes looking ahead to fall, to another school year and the chance to prove himself at football. But most of his thoughts, surely, were focused on a return to his beloved Michigan once school had ended. Much change was coming. Winter had frozen more than the ground. It had frozen time, seemingly, but now time and fate were thawing.

At the lakeshore the air is cool, but the wind has gone off to scour some other shore and the lake itself is quiet, a gentle surf ruffling the sand.

"What's it like," I ask Ernest. "The boat to Michigan."

"It's a ferry," he says.

"The ferry. What's it like?"

He laughs.

"I was seasick the very first time."

"Really? You, Hem?"

"I was just a little boy, Meelie."

"And now? Does it still make you queasy?"

"No. I like it now. I go to the bow and watch for the far shore when it's time."

"The Michigan shore."

"I watch for the bay—and Harbor Springs."

"That's where you land?"

"And from there we take a short train ride to Petoskey and then out to Walloon Lake and then a lake steamer to the cottage."

"Another steamer?"

"A small one. It's a short ride—chug, chug, chug and we're there!"

"It's an adventure."

Ernest grins.

"That's what makes it so great—so stupendous!"

"And the cottage is home away from home," I say.

"I guess it is. It's a different world up there."

"And how did your parents come to choose the place?"

"Well, it's a safe beach," he says.

"Safe?"

"No drop-off into deeper water. They were thinking ahead for us kids."

"Practical," I say. "And what is it like around the cottage?"

He shrugs.

"It's next to a farm—the Bacon farm. And Murphy's Point is just to the north. We camp there sometimes. It's all good country, believe me. The best country."

"I do believe you, Hem. It sounds lovely. And soon enough you go."

Ernest smiles, but then frowns.

"When do you leave Chicago, Meelie?"

My turn to shrug shoulders.

"Any time after school ends, of course. But maybe we'll stay a little longer."

"And then off to college?"

"Perhaps not right away. There's a matter of money to be resolved."

"Money sure does complicate things," he says.

We both stare out at the calm waters. I look for ships but none are in sight. The water seems to go on forever.

"Pretty nice out there today," he says. "But that changes fast. A storm can come up sudden."

"But not today, Hem. Today is—perfect."

"The storms are for other days, Meelie."

We walk along the lakeshore for a distance and then back up the beach and across the road and find a place to sit in a grove of trees.

"Do you keep up with the war?" I ask.

"Just in the papers. I read about the zeppelins bombing England."

"It hasn't been a quick affair at all, has it, Hem."

"No. You were right about that, Meelie. Last year you said it wouldn't be quick and would spread. Russia, the Turks—everyone is in it."

"Not everyone," I say.

Ernest looks at me a moment.

"We're neutral," he says. "President Wilson wants to keep us out of it."

"That's all well and good if he can do it," I say.

"If we get in, I might have to go," he says.

"Are you so sure?"

"What else would I do?"

"Then I'll pray we don't get in."

He nods, frowns. Clearly the war has to be on his mind as he grows into being a man. I fear that the war, which looks to last a long time, will snatch him up. I fear America will yet find itself in the middle of it. I hope I'm wrong. But war is a fire that spreads and consumes.

"What do you want to be, Meelie?" he says abruptly, the war already a fading memory. I'm glad for the change of subject.

"I don't know yet."

"Any clues?"

"Someone accomplished, of course."

"But what?" he says.

"Do I have to decide now?" I say playfully, tacking on a smile.

"Will you decide in college?"

"Yes—I suppose I will."

"I guess that's what college is for," he says, looking off a moment at the lake. "But does anything come to mind?"

"Persistent today, aren't we, Hem?"

"Just curious, Meelie. I face the same choices soon enough. I think about these things sometimes."

"You should," I say. "Will you go to college, Hemingstein? Down to Illinois, like you mentioned?"

"How about Cornell?"

"Cornell? Why not. If that's what you want."

"And if it isn't?" he says.

"Then perhaps Illinois."

"My dad wants me to go to Oberlin, in Ohio," he says flatly.

"Why Oberlin?"

"That's where *he* went," he says. "So did Uncle Tyler."

"And does he want you to become a doctor, too?"

"I'm sure he does."

"I suppose most doctors would prefer their sons be doctors, too. A natural thought."

"I don't think I'm cut out for that," he says.

"What does Grace say?"

"She wants me to follow rules and love God."

He adds a healthy smirk after a second or two.

"What do you think you want to do, Hem?"

"I'd like to see some of the world, Meelie."

"Doctors can see the world."

"What if I don't want to go to college at all?"

"What would Grace say to that?"

"Don't tell her, for God's sake," he says.

"Never. But if you don't go to college, what would you do instead?"

"I don't know. But it'll come to me, right?"

"I suspect it will," I say. "You have time yet."

"But it goes fast, right?"

"It has for me," I say.

"I guess time is slower for me."

"It will speed up soon enough, Hem."

He pauses and glances down into the water, then back up at me.

"Let's go eat," he says.

"Our little diner?"

"It never fails us, does it?"

We walked back to the diner and sat in a booth and it was good to take off my coat and feel the warmth and hear the clanging silverware and the din of conversations. We tried the spaghetti, which was good, though perhaps not as good—not as flavorful, perhaps, or spicy—as at the Italian restaurant we ate in the previous fall on State Street. There was fresh bread, though, and Ernest and I sopped up spaghetti sauce with it and buttered it, quite the feast.

After lunch we walked south on Michigan Avenue and stopped at the bridge across the Chicago River. Ernest found several pebbles and we tried to see how far we could skip them along the river.

"The pebbles are symbols," he says. "We throw them as far as we can and then the river current moves them along slowly—like fate."

"Destiny," I say.

"Yes. Destiny."

Soon my destiny will turn a corner, I hope. And soon enough, it will do the same for Ernest. We both gaze out at the river for a moment. It moves slowly. But steadily. Life moves slowly, but steadily.

"Time to go, Hem."

"I know. Me, too."

We hug warmly. In the embrace I can feel he has grown, is growing. He's not so much of the boy I met the year before. I wonder how I have changed, too. I'm sure I have. But it all comes to us slowly. And steadily, like the flowing river.

"I'll write in a few days, Hem."

"You better."

"Do you truly like the letters?"

"Of course. I love them. And now I like writing, too."

"You have much to say, I think. Maybe it's just a matter of letting it out."

"The more I read, the more I think about writing, Meelie."

"Maybe there's a lesson in that."

"Maybe. You never know."

"Now—off with you, Hemingstein. Mother awaits me."

"My best to her," he says.

"And mine to your father. And Grace."

This time I'm the one who lingers by the bridge, and as Ernest lumbers away he glances back once, smiles, and waves.

## Currents of Time

I wrote to Ernest several days after we visited the lake:

Greetings, Hemingstein,

And how is the weather out in Oak Park? And your family is well? It's looking like quite the lovely day here as I write you. Every day it seems the spring becomes bolder and decides it really will stay and blossom. Do you believe so? It was quite windy here yesterday, but today the wind has gone back to sleep, it seems—planning a surprise somewhere else, no doubt. And soon we will be able to walk without coats and we will feel—liberated. Light as feathers! We can go back to the lake and watch the waves fall and break and even walk along the sand barefoot, I suppose. If we choose to do that—we can! Stupendous!

I am counting the time before school ends. It's just around the corner, really, and I am excited by the prospect. Can you believe it? I scarcely can sometimes. But perhaps I should not count time, though. Perhaps I should just let time come as it will and allow it to wash over me and not try to manage time—control time. Like those pebbles we threw into the Chicago River, perhaps I should just let the currents of time move me along. But you know how much I want to be part of the wider world in some profound way. I just don't know how yet. We share that, dear Hemingstein. We will attain it, too. Don't you think? I do think so. I long for the next chapter, a new chapter.

Write back, dear Hemingstein, and let us plan some mischief about the city.

Meelie.

Hem's reply:

And greetings back to you, Meelie.

The exalted Hemingstein wishes you a stupendous day.

Stupendous!

The weather here is fine. No wind for days. But it will come back and find us. It always does. And then it summers somewhere else for the most part before returning.

The talk here is of Michigan. The clan must make its annual invasion north soon enough.

Oh—the news, Meelie. A baby brother has come and he is a loud little fellow, too!

Stupendous!

And a relief to all.

It seems the grand little gent is to go by the name Leicester.

That's a long name for such a short fellow.

He has the house in an uproar. And soon enough he will uproot us all up at Windemere, I suppose. The girls fuss over him and I wish he would get older already!

Maybe he will grow up to be—stupendous!

Can you meet the following Sunday at the diner? Write me right away and say you will.

Hemingstein.

I did write back right away and congratulated Ernest on his new baby brother. How excited he must be. His fears over their age difference will surely ease as Leicester grows and they can truly become brothers. I wonder what sort of older brother he would be.

After checking on Mother I set off on a Sunday morning for downtown. The sun is out and the air has a slightly cool tinge to it, but it was not really cold and I knew the sun would thaw the chill quickly enough and I would not then need my coat. Birds chattered happily in elm trees and a plump red cardinal sat contentedly on a low branch outside our building as though just then discovering the art of relaxing on a branch. The walk was pleasant and, as I walked, I enjoyed seeing other people embracing the lightness of a new spring after enduring the heaviness of winter.

All along Michigan Avenue people strolled and some hurried and I caught snatches of conversation as I passed by the clumps of people, or pairs of animated people – and one gentleman was even talking to himself! Talk about a one-sided argument! But he smiled as I passed and even tipped his hat. Perhaps he had good reason to talk only to himself. It was too lovely a day to quarrel over such things.

I reached the diner and Ernest was late, which was unexpected. Where was Hemingstein? The lumbering boy was nowhere to be seen. I had gotten so used to seeing him waiting, standing guard outside the diner like those lovely bronze lions at the art institute. Several times I looked both ways along the avenue for him and I began to worry he would not come. But soon I spotted his familiar face emerge from a clump of people from the south and his magnificent grin appeared and he waved happily.

Stupendous!

He reaches me a little out of breath.

"Meelie – sorry to be late."

"But you're not late. You arrived when you were supposed to."

"That's one way to look at it."

"It's the only way to look at it, Hem."

"Did you learn that in school?"

"No. Just something I heard. But it meshes nicely with our talks on fate, don't you think?"

"I suppose. Next time I'll slow down—since I'll still be on time."

"Now you're getting in the spirit of it, Hem."

"I'm spirited alright."

"But not a ghost."

"Maybe a hungry ghost. Let's eat."

"Even as a ghost—you'd be hungry, Hem."

"But ghosts don't gain weight. They can eat all they want."

"But do ghosts have stomachs?" I say.

"Do they even have mouths?" he says and we burst into laughter and go inside the diner to eat.

After a hearty early lunch we elect to visit the lake again. It's a short walk and I want to see it as many times as I can before leaving town. The lake is a little rougher this time and the waves are noticeable. I see a steamer out on the lake, dark smoke spurting from its stacks.

"Headed north," Ernest says, watching the steamer lumber along.

"And soon so shall you, Hemingstein."

He grins, obviously playing the coming trip in his head all the way to his beloved Walloon Lake.

We walk a ways, dodging the water as it creeps up the sand. Soon, from the north, there's an odd sound overhead. The sound of a motor. At first I wonder if somehow it comes from the city, perhaps from atop a building, but as we squint and shield our eyes to look up, we see it—an aircraft. It is flying quite low, perhaps only a hundred feet or so above the lake and only a few hundred yards out from shore. A giant buzzing insect. It flies past us, headed south. Later in life I would learn it was a Curtiss Flying Boat. We watch it until it is a tiny speck and then nothing at all.

"Stupendous!" Ernest finally declares and we both laugh and I slap his arm lightly.

"Everything is stupendous to you, Hem."

"Flying would be pretty stupendous alright," he says. "What do you think?"

I arch my eyebrows, but I'm not sure why.

"I've seen them before, Hem. I saw one at a state fair, when I was ten or eleven. What's the fuss?"

"What's the fuss?" he says, eyes widening a little. "It's flying, Meelie. Up in the air."

He extends his arms as though they are wings and twirls around once, rather clumsily.

"Is that flying, Hem?"

"Should I flap my arms to convince you?"

"Go ahead."

He does and looks like a great clumsy bird with no chance of flying at all and I laugh at him and he breaks into laughter, too.

"Maybe if I jump when I flap," he says, laughing hard again and nearly falling down in the sand.

"You keep flapping, Hem. You'll get somewhere yet."

"If I could," he says, "I'd flap all the way to Walloon Lake. Imagine that, Meelie. Up in the air, looking down at the shoreline, the trees. Looking over at geese and ducks and how surprised they must be to see someone flying."

"You start flapping and I'll give you a push and we'll see if you clear the first waves, Hem."

"I need something higher," he says. "One of the buildings on Michigan Avenue ought to do the trick."

"Well, if you leap from a building, it had better be by the Chicago River."

"Even then, it likely wouldn't turn out so good," he says.

"No flying for you, Hem. Not today, anyway. And I won't let you near those buildings."

"What about you, Meelie?"

"Me? No interest. I'll stay firmly rooted here to the ground."

"What about that one you saw at the fair."

"What about it?"

"Wasn't it exciting?"

"Maybe for the pilot," I say. "It was just wire and wood. And all rather haphazard and such, Hem. A contraption."

"A woman pilot," he says. "That would be something."

"It would," I say. "Indeed. But not me."

"Why not?"

"Hem—do you plan to make me leap from that building with you?"

"How fast can you flap your arms, Meelie?"

"Not fast enough, I'd say."

"Still, flying would be swell," he says.

"Have you ever done it?"

"Not yet," he says. "But some day."

"I think I prefer solid land under my feet, Hem. Or at least the solid deck of a ship. Not so far to fall."

"You would like the trip to Harbor Springs, Meelie."

"Maybe I would."

"You could come up," he says. "This summer."

I look out over the waves at the horizon. I think of school almost done and then it will be time to leave Chicago and go back to family first, in Kansas City.

"But where would I stay, Hem? The Hemingway clan is a small army."

"We are," he says, smirking. "But there's room. Some of us would camp out. We do it all the time."

"Because you're an army," I say. "I'm not much of a camper, I'm afraid."

"You wouldn't have to be. We'd set you up fine. All the comforts of home plus great country and food."

I smile but say nothing.

"Would you consider it, Meelie?"

"I don't know. I don't know when we will be leaving Chicago, Hem. That's set, you realize. Just a matter of time."

"I know," he says, glancing at the lake. "But you said yourself you might stay for a time after school is over. That's perfect to make the trip up to Michigan."

I look again out at the water, the horizon. The little steamer is far off now and soon will be out of sight. It suddenly looks quite lonely out there on the lake.

"Maybe," I say. "I don't know."

"But you'll consider it?"

I look at his face, so expectant.

"I'll consider it, of course."

"Good." He seems satisfied for now.

"Let's walk back, Hem. When I get home I'll even see how Mother views such a trip. But no promises. You must understand."

Ernest nods.

"Nothing's guaranteed," he says solemnly.

We stroll back leisurely and finally reach the bridge over the Chicago River, which seems to always be our point of departure. For all my life I think I will remember the view of the river from the bridge and the slow-moving water and the buildings along Michigan Avenue and the sounds of motorcars and people.

"Time to part," he says. He knows the routine well.

"My best to your family—congratulate all on little Leicester."

"I will."

We hug.

"Stay away from tall buildings, and don't flap your arms, Hem."

He grins.

"I promise."

"We'll leave all this flying business to other people," I say.

"Think about my invitation," he says.

"I'll give it every consideration, Hemingstein."

I turn and head south, toward Hyde Park. I don't look back and vaguely I wonder if Ernest does.

# Bloody Dawn

*The assault began at dawn.*

*Dozens of crabs.*

*A raiding party.*

*No – more than that.*

*Much more.*

*An execution squad.*

*Assassins.*

*Banners fluttering.*

*Like I had seen by the lagoon.*

*Their leaders in gold and silver crab armor.*

*Exhorting them into the fray.*

*They caught me napping.*

*And dry.*

*From lack of water.*

*And lack of strength.*

*Lack of will.*

*They came in several waves.*

*More than ever before.*

*Snip.*

*Cut.*

*Gouge.*

*Bleed.*

*And at first.*

*It seemed a dream.*

*Not the glorious dreams of Chicago.*

*With Hem.*

*But the dreams before the dawn.*

*When I am back on the island.*

*On Amelia Island.*

*And Hem's face is fading.*

*His grin fading.*

*The magnificent grin.*

*Fading.*

*Chicago's buildings – fading.*

*The Chicago River and Lake Michigan.*

*Are fading.*

*And the heat of the island.*

*Amelia's Island.*

*Has not yet.*

*Not quite.*

*Not fully.*

*Enveloped me again.*

*Drenched me.*

*And my eyes flutter.*

*My dry lips quiver.*

*But still there is hope.*

*That I will wake.*

*In the air.*

*In the Electra.*

*Or at home, in Atchison.*

*A girl.*

*Just a young girl.*

*In my own comfy bed.*

*Or I will awake.*

*In Hyde Park.*

*And see it's time.*

*To dress and prepare.*

*And walk north to downtown.*

*To see Hem.*

*And the magnificent grin.*

*And the wondrous Lake Michigan.*

*And hear about.*

*The mystery land.*

*Across the lake.*

*And well north.*

*The land of Walloon Lake.*

*And Harbor Springs.*

*And Petoskey.*

*Places far better than here.*

*Places with far better names than here.*

*Amelia Island.*

*It's just a name.*

*Somehow I manage.*

*To fend off the crab legions.*

*And then move.*

*First, to stand.*

*Then to wade into the surf.*

*And allow the salt's bite.*

*To cleanse my wounds.*

*And then I go into the shade of trees.*

*To catch my breath.*

*And wonder:*

*Will there be water today?*

*There wasn't yesterday.*

*In the shade I sit.*

*Back against a palm tree trunk.*

*A section of palm frond.*

*In my hand.*

*My spear.*

*Like Spartans at the pass.*

*Thermopylae.*

*Leonidas and his men.*

*They faced legions, too.*

*Not Roman legions.*

*Barbarian legions.*

*Did quite well.*

*As I recall.*

*Until they all died.*

*In a shower of arrows.*

*A thought:*

*Is it my birthday?*

# Spitballs Again

*Open up, dear portal of time, and let me slip through once more:*

A few letters passed between Ernest and me for some weeks, and when next I saw him we went back to Weeghman Park, back to the world of Mr. Claude Hendrix and his infamous and vaunted spitball. The season was still young and on this day the Chicago Whales, as last season's Chicago Federals were now named, faced the Brooklyn Tip-Tops. The names tickled me. Very funny names. In this league there were also the St. Louis Terriers and the Kansas City Packers, which I told Ernest I must root for since they were from Kansas City, and also the Pittsburgh Rebels and Buffalo Buffeds. Perhaps the team name that made us laugh above all—the Newark Peppers.

It is fine May weather at Weeghman Park, the sun out, but not blazing at all. The breeze is inconsequential. It has rained the day before and the field was damp in the morning, but the sun dried it quickly. The standsare full of thousands of chattering people. Players hefte bats and smash fists into gloves and stomp their feet in the infield dirt. Soldiers preparing for battle, I suppose. Some of the players wave to women in the stands and the ladies seem quite thrilled by it all.

"Will Mr. Hendrix be as coy about his spitball as before, Hem?"

"Of course. That's his job."

"I thought his job was to throw the ball to the crouching man."

"Pitch the ball."

"Pitch," I say. "With saliva on it."

"And the crouching man is a catcher," he says.

"Makes sense," I say. "And of course the batter tries to intervene in the relationship between Mr. Hendrix and his crouching catcher."

"Pretty great, isn't it?" he says.

"Delightful, Hem. Picturesque. And the saliva is an added attraction."

"It's just part of the game, Meelie. Like I told you, everybody does it."

"But perhaps not as well as Mr. Hendrix."

"He's pretty good alright."

"That's comforting," I say.

"Don't you like baseball, Meelie?"

"I like it fine. It certainly has its colorful characters."

"Baseball's like a play," he says. "It's a drama."

"And here I thought it was a sport, Hem."

"You know what I mean."

I watch the game differently than Ernest does, I suspect. He absorbs the energy and cheers from the fans and perhaps sees the players as noble knights facing a dreaded foe. A contest to be won to affirm honor. A contest reflecting the vigors of life. I watch the flight of the ball when it's thrown or hit and contemplate the physics of it all. By doing that, baseball becomes interesting to me and even somewhat relaxing to witness. It's a good day indeed for the Whales, whose uniform jerseys have a large letter C encircling a whale. They win this day over the Brooklyn Tip-Tops, 9-2. But it's unclear to me how a whale inspires baseball.

After the game thousands of people noisily spill out of Weeghman Park, and for a time we are carried along with them, a huge wave of humanity that crests and falls and finally dissipates. Like water, people, too seek their own level. Hem and I walk along Michigan Avenue headed south.

"We must eat now, of course," I say. "You must be famished."

"I could eat."

"You can always eat, Hemingstein."

"It's one of my talents."

"We all must have talents," I say. "Mr. Claude Hendrix surely does."

"And what are your talents, Meelie? Besides needling Mr. Claude Hendrix, that is."

"I'm smart, Hem. Oh, not a genius. Not like that. But I'm smart. I can learn. I like learning."

"Me, too."

"How's the reading going, Hem?"

"I keep at it. Sometimes I think I can put words together pretty well, too. But it's hard, writing. I can see that."

"You must work at it," I say. "I'm sure Shakespeare had to get started somewhere."

"Mr. Shakespeare was maybe just born to it," he says. "Some people are."

"Maybe you are, Hem."

"Like Mr. Claude Hendrix was born to spitballing?" he says.

We laugh.

"Some day people will look back and say, 'That Claude Hendrix was really some spitballer.' That will be his enduring legacy, Hem."

"What will be ours?"

"We can't know that yet," I say.

"But we can speculate."

"It does no good, speculation."

"Oh, sure it does, Meelie. Everyone must have dreams."

"Dreams are fine. As long as they don't consume."

"But if we don't dream," he says, "how do we discover what we want to be?"

"I think we know it when we see it."

"Have you seen it yet, Meelie?"

"No," I say. "Not yet."

"Me neither."

"It will come. We have to be patient."

"Like Mr. Claude Hendrix loading up his spitball."

"Hemingstein!"

"Well, you have to admit—he's pretty stupendous at it."

"The Shakespeare of spitballs," I say. "Stupendous!"

"Or maybe the Houdini of spitballs."

"Why Houdini?"

"Because you never quite catch him at it."

"Good, Hem."

"Have you ever seen Houdini, Meelie?"

"Just photos."

"His eyes are very strange," he says. "Spooky eyes."

"Maybe that's just a pose. He's an entertainer."

"Could be," he says. "Much of life seems to be a pose."

"Profound, Hem. Do you think that's so?"

"I think people need to play characters, be characters."

"Like in a novel?" I say.

"Exactly like in a novel. When we read, we try to figure out who they are. Sometimes we don't know that for sure because *they* don't know for sure."

"Insightful, Hem."

"And so they pose, Meelie, because they don't know for sure who they are, and it's easier, or more comfortable, to pose."

Have I been posing, I wonder? Am I the lonely girl in Hyde Park who doesn't make friends at school? The solitary girl who cares for her mother and sees neither left or right and only straight ahead? Nonsense. I have a plan that starts beyond school and Hyde Park. And I have Hem as my good friend. And I have seen much of Chicago thanks to our friendship.

"Well, let's pose as diners, Hem, and go to our little diner."

"Stupendous!"

At the diner we feast on fried chicken and mashed potatoes saturated in beef gravy, and there's some creamed corn and even tart applesauce. I am very hungry and eat more than usual, but the food is delicious and it feels so very good to eat well and to be full.

At the bridge over the river we linger as usual to watch the river flow, to watch small boats bobbing gently on the surface.

"Have you thought about my invitation, Meelie? To come up to Walloon Lake?"

"Of course, Hem. I said I would think it over."

"How's the thinking going?"

"I said I would give it every consideration."

"You would love it up there."

"I'm sure I would. I love seeing new places."

"Then you should come up."

"I have to weigh everything, Hem. I have to consider mother's needs, too."

"But she could do without you a few days, couldn't she?"

"I don't know. I haven't mentioned it to her yet."

"Would she mind if you went?"

"I don't know. But I promise to talk to her about it. Soon."

"School's almost over," he says. "We go north soon."

"Isn't it glorious? I'm so glad."

"And so you should come see us," he says.

"Maybe. It's quite the journey, you must admit."

"A ride on a steamer, Meelie."

"And a second steamer on your lake, remember? "I say.

"That's a short trip."

"And then the whole Hemingway clan—an army."

"But a friendly army."

"Are you a salesman, Hem?"

"No, but Walloon Lake is easy to sell."

"I have no doubt."

"So, come visit."

"I'll write you on it, Hem. I promise. This week."

"You better."

"But I shall. Now, hug me and we go home to family."

It's a warm and lingering embrace. Hem smells like soap, but it's a pleasant smell.

I turn south and walk. I resist glancing back, but finally do: Ernest is looking down at the river.

## Fading Light

*No more water, it seems.*

*I have found none.*

*No rain.*

*How long?*

*Not sure.*

*The mind plays tricks.*

*I have looked everywhere.*

*Everywhere I can reach, that is.*

*With weak legs.*

*And a weak mind?*

*No.*

*Again – no.*

*I can't let the mind go.*

*It's the source of all power.*

*It can make the legs go again.*

*Well, with water.*

*But there is none.*

*The crooks of trees are dry.*

*Have I checked them all?*

*Impossible.*

*Is it?*

*Of course.*

*Be sensible.*

*I am sensible.*

*Are you really?*

*Yes.*

*And how would you know?*

*I just would.*

*That must be comforting.*

*Nothing is comforting.*

*Except water.*

*More valuable than gold.*

*But there is none.*

*And so I wait.*

*For rain.*

*Rain I think will not come.*

*And for the light.*

*To fade.*

*Below the horizon.*

## Sweet Sorrow

*Off to the past I go:*

And so the days of fun and adventure were coming to an end. Sadly, I wrote Ernest that I could not visit him in Michigan. I simply couldn't leave Mother for such a long time, no matter how interesting it would be. I knew it would be a great adventure with Ernest, who makes everything seem more alive by his presence and enthusiasm. Life for me was taking a turn, though, an important turn, an inevitable turn, and the Chicago days were fading fast. But I knew enough Shakespeare to realize that parting was indeed the sweet sorrow and could be quite painful.

I made my way to the docks and the steamer bound for Harbor Springs, Michigan. The sun was out with no clouds. A beautiful day for a boat ride. The Hemingway clan arrived almost as I did. Ernest and I shook hands, a hug seeming to be inappropriate in front of his parents. The Hemingways had a number of large luggage trunks and it was very much a grand expedition and even sort of like a military mission. They had come into Chicago by train and all seemed eager to board the steamer and go up the lake.

After the family was aboard the steamer, Ernest and I lingered on the docks. I knew this would likely be the last time I ever saw my young and dear friend. He knew it, too. Life was taking us in different directions. Life moves people around likes pawns on chess boards. But fate dictates that it happens.

"I wish you were coming along, Meelie."

"I know, Hem. And it would be such fun."

"It would," he says, his eyes moistening. He looks at the steamer a moment and then back to me.

"Once you get to Walloon Lake, you won't miss me," I say.

"But I will. You know I will." He looks quite hurt.

"Yes—I know. I'll miss you, too, Hem. Who will I visit the diner with now?"

"Take your mother, Meelie. Eat Michigan blueberries and think of me."

"I'll do that," I say. "And it would be good for her to get out."

He takes off his cap and brushes his hair back with a hand.

"When do you leave Chicago, Meelie?"

"Soon. It will take some time to get Mother organized. But soon."

Ernest looks up at the steamer again. People hurry by us as they make their way up on deck.

"You must go, Hemingstein."

"I know." He looks down a moment. When he looks up tears stream from his eyes and mine become moist, too. I extend my arms and we hug.

"Take good care of yourself, Hemingstein."

"You, too, Meelie."

The hug lingers and is warm. I feel his breath on my neck.

"Enjoy Walloon Lake while you have it," I say. "Life flows faster than we ever realize."

"I know it," he says. He looks into my eyes. "Make more friends, Meelie. See more of the world."

"I intend to, Hem. I've learned a lot this past year, from you, about seeing the world."

His smile quickly becomes the magnificent grin, a grin I shall remember all my days. He turns to go up on deck, but after a few steps he stops and turns back to me.

"We're going places, Meelie—the both of us."

"I think so, too, Hem."

"And we'll hear about each other," he says. "Do you believe that?"

"I do. With all my heart."

His lips tremble.

"I love you, Meelie."

"I love you, too, Hem. Now off with you. Mustn't keep family waiting."

He allows the magnificent grin to spread as wide as I have ever seen it.

"Stupendous!" he shouts.

I laugh.

"Stupendous, Hemingstein!"

For just a few seconds he lingers there, looking down at me, the grin not receding even a little, and then his face disappears for the last time and I wait patiently on the docks as the steamer pulls away and I watch it until I can't see it at all and then I go home and ask Mother what she would like to have for lunch.

# Ascension

*My eyes are barely open.*

*Can barely stay open.*

*I force them open.*

*They resist.*

*But oblige.*

*They creak open.*

*Under protest.*

*Rusty doors.*

*And see the horizon.*

*It's dawn, yet hot already.*

*Barely dawn.*

*Just as I.*

*Barely.*

*Can see.*

*But I see well enough.*

*To know nothing is out there.*

*Nothing is here.*

*Nothing is everywhere.*

*And nowhere is water to be found.*

*How long without water?*

*Long enough.*

*Too long.*

*But long enough.*

*My throat – do I have a throat?*

*I can't feel it.*

*Or so it seems.*

*Or maybe it's my hands that do not feel.*

*Or maybe it's just the mind.*

*Playing tricks.*

*Numb.*

*Again.*

*It's all that still works.*

*The mind.*

*Barely.*

*And so it seems.*

*I have run out of gas.*

*Twice.*

*Once in the Electra.*

*And now as Amelia.*

*On Amelia Island.*

*The sun will become brutal soon.*

*So I crawl.*

*Pathetically.*

*Slowly.*

*A wounded snake.*

*To the shade of palms.*

*But with a view of the ocean.*

*And horizon.*

*The horizon.*

*Oh beautiful horizon.*

*Where I long to be.*

*Anywhere but here.*

*I tilt my head.*

*Toward the sky.*

*Blue, blue, blue sky.*

*No clouds.*

*Flying weather.*

*And I chuckle.*

*Though it hurts my throat.*

*Not a chuckle – a rattle.*

*A chuckle.*

*A true chuckle.*

*Is no longer possible.*

*So I rattle.*

*And look again up at flying weather.*

*And know I will fly again.*

*Soon.*

*Without doubt.*

*All is clear enough now.*

*Very soon.*

*But first I think.*

*All the way back.*

*All the way to the beginning.*

*Or where it begins for me.*

*Which is far back enough.*

*And then I go forward.*

*Lingering at times.*

*On this memory.*

*That memory.*

*Many sweet memories.*

*Flying with Neta.*

*Dinners with family.*

*The good days.*

*The early days.*

*Wonderful days.*

*Days gone by.*

*Oh, to join them again.*

*A thought:*

*Oh, what are memories?*

*Are they real?*

*Photographic?*

*Factual?*

*Honest?*

*Or are they just how we want to remember events?*

*Are we afraid of the past?*

*And have to manipulate it?*

*I don't know.*

*I think we must accept our memories.*

*Trust them.*

*Hope they are real.*

*Mine seem real enough.*

*In this unreal world.*

*Wait – it's real enough.*

*It's just the consequences.*

*That seem unreal.*

*So unexpected.*

*Well, at first unexpected.*

*Now – inevitable.*

*Oh, sad inevitability.*

*I can barely think the word.*

*So many syllables.*

*But don't think of syllables.*

*Then think of what?*

*Think of what went wrong.*

*Nothing went wrong.*

*Really?*

*Nothing?*

*It wasn't one thing.*

*It was many things.*

*What things?*

*I don't know.*

*What don't you know?*

*Why this happened.*

*That's what I don't know.*

*Does it matter?*

*Knowing is my last luxury.*

*What do you want to know?*

*How I got here.*

*You ran out of gas, girl.*

*Or maybe just ran out of luck.*

*Maybe.*

*Gas.*

*Luck.*

*Run out of one and you've run out of the other.*

*Indeed.*

*My throat rattles again.*

*And so.*

*There is no truth to be found.*

*In this matter, anyway.*

*That's right, girl.*

*You took off.*

*And shouldn't have.*

*But you did.*

*Now you're here.*

*This is the result.*

*But it was certainly not the goal.*

*What was the goal?*

*Is that worth worry now?*

*Yes.*

*I must know.*

*But you cannot.*

*No – I must.*

*That chance has gone, girl.*

*Gone where?*

*Just gone.*

*Where – no longer matters.*

*Where – there is no more where.*

*That's silly.*

*No.*

*It's true.*

*Maybe.*

*Yes – it's true.*

*I must accept it.*

*And accept inevitability.*

*That word again.*

*A wordy word.*

*That makes me chuckle – rattle.*

*Ernest would appreciate that.*

*Dear Ernest.*

*Hem.*

*Hemingstein.*

*Stupendous!*

*He became a man of words.*

*Many words.*

*Where is Ernest now?*

*Far from Oak Park.*

*Famous.*

*Like me.*

*Luckier.*

*Than I.*

*Oh how I would cherish.*

*The sight of his magnificent grin.*

*Over coffee.*

*At our little diner.*

*On Michigan Avenue.*

*And I would cherish.*

*Ernest flapping his arms.*

*Pretending to fly.*

*By the lake.*

*Lake Michigan.*

*And now I am.*

*The one.*

*Who pretended.*

*To fly.*

*Well.*

*Did my best.*

*I can say that.*

*It wasn't enough.*

*But that matters not.*

*Not now.*

*And so there is one last act.*

*I pull myself up.*

*Back against the palm trunk.*

*For a better look.*

*At the ocean.*

*At the horizon.*

*Up at the blue flying weather.*

*And then I see them.*

*The crabs.*

*All their legions.*

*The multitudes.*

*Banners streaming.*

*Their armor gleaming in the sun.*

*They come up from the beach.*

*Out of the trees.*

*From all directions.*

*They mass and the mass grows.*

*Until it seems.*

*Crabs cover.*

*Every grain.*

*Of sand.*

*And then they advance.*

*It's the final charge.*

*The day of reckoning.*

*I watch them come.*

*And catch my breath.*

*I smile.*

*Because I have that choice.*

*One of the final choices.*

*And I look far past.*

*The blue sky.*

*Into the galaxy.*

*Because I have that choice, too.*

*And close my eyes.*

*And exhale what's left.*

*And deny the crabs the kill.*

*I ascend.*

*I leave.*

*I leave only my dry body behind.*

*And rise.*

*Up, up, up.*

*Oh, the sky is blue, blue, blue.*

*And I'm in the Canary again.*

*And I am The Canary.*

*Once again.*

*And forever.*

# Epilogue

*New York City*

*July, 1937*

It was sunny and already a warm morning. The sidewalks were jammed with busy people. A sea of men in hats and ladies in colorful dresses—reds, yellows, purples. The New York Yankees were well on their way to a ninth pennant. Joe DiMaggio would hit .346 and Lou Gehrig .351. A group of well-dressed men were chatting happily about the Yankees as Ernest Hemingway walked past them on Fifth Avenue. He heard the baseball chatter and smiled. It reminded him of baseball games in Chicago when he was a boy—the Chicago Whales and later the Cubs. In those days Wrigley Field was first called Weeghman Park.

Ernest felt good. Work on the *Spanish Earth* was going well. Now he was thinking about where to have lunch. At a corner he heard two young women talking, but their words were lost on him until one said, "Amelia Earhart—isn't it just so sad?"

"Excuse me," Ernest said to the young woman. "Did something happen to Amelia Earhart?"

The woman wiped a tear from her cheek.

"I guess you haven't heard," she said.

"Heard what?"

"She's gone," the woman said. "Crashed in the ocean. You didn't know?"

"No, I didn't," Ernest said faintly, suddenly feeling sick. "When?"

"Yesterday, I think. Or the day before. I'm not sure. We heard about it on the radio just a while ago."

The two women smiled politely as best they could and then crossed the street. Ernest stood at the corner, his hands thrust into his pants pockets, staring across the street, but not really seeing what was there. Soon he became aware again of people passing him on both sides, and he crossed the street and went into the first bar he came to, sat on a stool and ordered a whiskey. There were only a few men at the end of the bar and several in booths. The bartender brought him his drink and went back to washing glasses.

Ernest tried to capture an image of Amelia from 1915 in his head, but it would not quite come into sharp focus. He was still shocked by the news. Soon a man came in and sat a couple stools from him. The man, young and thin, ordered a drink and spread open a copy of the *New York Times* on the bar. Ernest glanced at the paper several times.

"What's the news on Earhart?" he said quietly to the man.

"Not good. They're looking. But it's a big ocean."

"Yes. It is." Ernest drank the rest of his whiskey.

"A pretty sad deal," the man said. "Maybe she bit off too much."

Ernest felt anger flash throughout him, but he suppressed it.

"We don't know what happened out there, friend," he said as evenly as he could.

"No, we don't." The man nodded. "We just know how it turned out."

Ernest turned away from the man and soon he remembered back to 1915, to the last time he saw Amelia, at the docks when he sailed to Michigan. A long time behind him. But now her smiling face was crystal clear in his head.

"Meelie," he whispered.

"What was that?" the man said.

"Nothing," Ernest said. "May I read the story?"

The man pushed the paper toward Ernest.

"Help yourself."

As Ernest read the story, it made him feel even worse.

"Thank you, friend," he told the man.

For a long moment Ernest sat then paid for his drink and walked out to the street. He walked without direction until he saw Central Park ahead. He crossed the street into the park and stood by a pond and gazed out at the calm water. Then memories came rushing back to him: the little diner on Michigan Avenue. Baseball games at Weeghman Park. The day Amelia came to his football game at Phipps Field. The picnics at Lake Michigan. Thanksgiving dinner with his family in Oak Park. Their good-byes on the lake.

Tears rolled down his cheeks. He cried for a few moments, but managed to choke it off. He composed himself quickly, wiped his eyes, and looked around. A young woman walked by and smiled at him. On the ground he saw a pebble and he picked it up and hefted it in his hand a moment and then tossed it into the pond. He watched the ripples spread until they were gone.

"Good-bye, sweet Meelie," he said, and then he walked briskly out of the park and across Fifth Avenue toward his hotel.

**Michael Loyd Gray** was born in Jonesboro, Arkansas, but grew up in Champaign, Illinois. He earned a MFA in English from Western Michigan University and has taught at colleges and universities in upstate New York, Michigan, Illinois, Wisconsin, and Texas. He graduated from the University of Illinois with a journalism degree and was a newspaper staff writer in Arizona and Illinois for ten years, conducting the last interview with novelist Erskine Caldwell.

He is the winner of the 2005 Alligator Juniper Fiction Prize and the 2005 The Writers Place Award for Fiction. Gray's novel *Well Deserved* won the 2008 Sol Books Prose Series Prize. His novel *Not Famous Anymore* was awarded a grant by the Elizabeth George Foundation and was released by Three Towers Press in 2012. His novel *King Biscuit* was released in 2012 by Tempest Books.

Gray is a lifelong Chicago Bears and Rolling Stones fan and lives in Kalamazoo, Michigan. He teaches as full-time online English faculty for South University, where he is one of the founding editors of the literary journal *Asynchronous* and sponsor of an online readings series featuring fiction and poetry.

# Bottom Dog Press

## Books in the Harmony Series

*The Canary: A Novel*
by Michael Loyd Gray 192 pgs. $18
*The Harmonist at Nightfall: Poems of Indiana*
By Shari Wagner, 114 pgs. $16
*Painting Bridges: A Novel*
By Patricia Averbach, 234 pgs. $18
*Ariadne & Other Poems*
By Ingrid Swanberg, 120 pgs. $16
*The Search for the Reason Why: New and Selected Poems*
By Tom Kryss, 192 pgs. $16
*Kenneth Patchen: Rebel Poet in America*
By Larry Smith, Revised 2nd Edition, 326 pgs. Cloth $28
*Selected Correspondence of Kenneth Patchen,*
Edited with introduction by Allen Frost,
312 pgs. Paper $18/ Cloth $28
*Awash with Roses: Collected Love Poems of Kenneth Patchen*
Eds. Laura Smith and Larry Smith
With introduction by Larry Smith, 200 pgs. $16

* * * *

## Harmony Collections and Anthologies

*d.a.levy and the mimeograph revolution*
Eds. Ingrid Swanberg and Larry Smith, 276 pgs. $20
*Come Together: Imagine Peace*
Eds. Ann Smith, Larry Smith, Philip Metres, 204 pgs. $16
*Evensong: Contemporary American Poets on Spirituality*
Eds. Gerry LaFemina and Chad Prevost, 240 pgs. $16
*America Zen: A Gathering of Poets*
Eds. Ray McNiece and Larry Smith, 224 pgs. $16
*Family Matters: Poems of Our Families*
Eds. Ann Smith and Larry Smith, 232 pgs. $16

**Bottom Dog Press, Inc.**
PO Box 425/ Huron, Ohio 44839
Order Online at:
http://smithdocs.net

CPSIA information can be obtained at www.ICGtesting.com
Printed in the USA
BVOW08s1239160813

328705BV00002B/9/P

9 781933 964737